THE PRICE OF MEAT

Danny Penman was born near Liverpool in 1966. He graduated from Liverpool University in 1993 with a Ph.D. in biochemistry, and became a journalist after hitch-hiking through Central America at the height of its unrest. He worked for the *Independent* for two years before becoming a freelance environmental writer and broadcaster. While at the *Independent*, he covered the explosion in protests against live animal exports, new roads and car culture. Based in London, Danny Penman currently writes for the *Observer*, the *Independent* and the *Evening Standard*.

The Price of Meat

DANNY PENMAN

VICTOR GOLLANCZ

LONDON

First published in Great Britain 1996
by Victor Gollancz
An imprint of the Cassell Group
Wellington House, 125 Strand, London WC2R 0BB

A Gollancz Paperback Original

© Danny Penman 1996

The right of Danny Penman to be identified as author of
this work has been asserted by him in accordance with
the Copyright, Designs and Patents Act, 1988.

A catalogue record for this book is
available from the British Library.

ISBN 0 575 06344 0

Typeset by Textype Typesetters, Cambridge
Printed in Great Britain by Guernsey Press Co. Ltd,
Guernsey, Channel Isles

96 97 98   5 4 3 2 1

Dedicated to Jill Phipps,
who died while trying to stop
the export of veal calves.
And also to Mavis Penman.

Contents

Contents

Acknowledgements

First thanks must go to Mark Glover, of Respect for Animals, for inspiring this book. Many others have kindly helped and donated their valuable time and information throughout; Professor John Webster from Bristol University; Dr Tim O'Brien and Peter Stevenson from Compassion in World Farming; Professor Andrew Linzey from Oxford University; Penny Lewis, Peter Cox, Professor Stephen Clark from Liverpool University; Richard Ryder, Charlotte Morrissey, the RSPCA; Andrew Tyler, Mike Mendl and François Wemelsfelder of the Scottish Agriculture College; BioIndustry Association; Soil Association; Alan Long; Ron James of Pharmaceutical Proteins; David White of Imutran; Nick Scott-Ram; Stephen Dealler; Meat and Livestock Commission; and the British Poultry Meat Federation. Finally, this book would not have been possible without the tireless antics of Richard Otley, Roger Mills, and the boys from ITF.

The extract on pp. 140–41 from *The Restaurant at the End of the Universe* by Douglas Adams is reprinted with the permission of Pan Books.

Introduction

The day *may* come when the rest of the animal creation may
acquire those rights which never could have been withholden
from them but by the hand of tyranny.

Jeremy Bentham

Sussex Police thought they were in for an easy time. It was a
little after nine o'clock on a cold January evening and 400
people had gathered to protest about the export of live veal
calves to the Continent. Facing the predominantly middle-
aged, middle-class people were a hundred police officers. It
was a bitterly cold evening but there were worse places for
officers to patrol than the gates to the port of Shoreham in
West Sussex. But then something odd happened. A woman
shouted 'They're coming they're coming,' as a convoy of
eight trucks rolled into sight. The passive crowd erupted and
began tearing down the barricades. People pushed and
shoved past shocked police officers and sat in the road. The
trucks halted. Dozens of people scrambled onto the trucks
and the police struggled to stop them. One officer walked
away in tears after hearing the cries of the calves packed into
the trucks. A middle-aged woman was punched in the stomach by another policeman and lay twisting in pain on the
ground. A man in his twenties was knocked unconscious by
another policeman. Despite the crazed stampede there was

very little sound. Only the harsh breathing of the protesters and the cries of the animals could be heard above the silence.

The police tried and failed to pull demonstrators clear of the trucks. A woman in her sixties passed a lump of concrete to a man on the roof of the front truck. A windscreen shattered. Another was busily at work under the vehicle with a spanner. Its air brakes were disconnected and the convoy immobilized.

In a few short minutes the first veil protecting the farming industry from the public gaze was torn aside. People saw one aspect of it – live animal exports – and reacted. From then on it would take up to a thousand police, many wearing riot gear, to ensure that farmers could export their animals through Shoreham. The pattern was mirrored at ports and airports across Britain as the police battled to keep the exports moving while the protesters tried to stop them. It was their first glimpse of the farming industry and they didn't like what they saw.

The meat trade impinges on everyday life in every way, from the burger bar in the high street to the shoes on your feet, animal products are everywhere. Animals are central to human culture: we hunt them for fun, eat them for pleasure and poison their bodies for profit. This book focuses on the most common form of animal exploitation: meat production. That is not to say that fox-hunting or testing cosmetics on animals are insignificant or trivial forms of abuse, it means that the sheer scale of cruelty inflicted by the meat industry merits special attention. About 720 million creatures are killed each year for meat in Britain. About 2 million are used in experiments and many thousands are killed for so called 'sports' like hare-coursing and fox-hunting. Much has been written on these subjects and one more book would add little to the debate.

Many veils protect the farming industry, the most useful

being the countryside itself. It appears serene and many farm creatures seem to come and go as they wish. Who would guess that the cow is one of the most ill-treated creatures in Britain? She lives an apparently happy, carefree life just eating and sleeping all day. But this is an illusion. The drive to increase milk production siphons nutrients from her body and she is burnt out after about six years, well short of her natural lifespan.

Consider the pig, as intelligent as a family dog, confined to a crate so narrow it cannot even turn around. Or the chicken, which grows so fast that its legs break when it can no longer support its rapidly swelling body. Even sheep are pushed to their limits. The easiest way to boost meat production is to breed ewes that carry two or three lambs at a time, and this overloads their small bodies and ensures that millions of lambs die every year because their mothers cannot care for them properly.

Pushing animals beyond their biological limits is not just an issue for people who care about their fellow creatures; it is of concern to anyone who cares about their own health and well-being. Mad-cow disease, salmonella and listeria have all shown what happens when humanity tampers too much with the food supply. We may be lucky and mad-cow disease will only kill a few thousand people. But, more frighteningly, it may be only the first of many diseases, produced by the meat industry, to infect humans.

This book is also an exploration of how in the future animals will be genetically engineered for human gain. Some animals have been engineered with human growth-hormone genes to make them grow faster. Pigs have been bred with human genes to make them suitable organ donors. Scientists are also working on turning pigs and chickens into grazing animals. Sheep have been engineered to produce new drugs and others have been designed so that their fleeces fall off without the need for shearing. Animals may soon be engineered with lower intelligence so that they would be less aware of being exploited.

This book also explores the ethics of animal rights. All the issues raised will be explored within the context of the ethics of animal rights, and with the guiding thoughts of the country's most forward-thinking philosophers. It is not turgid: good philosophy is straightforward and intuitively obvious. When it is twisted to support the *status quo* then it becomes difficult to understand. Over the last three decades a radical new approach to human dealings with the rest of creation has begun to emerge from its roots in the last century. Animal rights – the belief that the lives of non-human creatures are also worthy of respect – will turn into one of the most important guiding forces of the next century and beyond.

This is not a book for vegetarians, although I hope they will find it useful; nor is it designed to shock, but it is shocking. Rather, it is a book for people who care about where their food comes from and how it is produced. It is a book that exposes the farming industry for what it is and it also proposes viable solutions. The first steps in the liberation of animals in Europe, at least, will come when the Treaty of Rome, the founding stone of the European Union, is amended to recognize that animals are thinking, feeling, sentient creatures. At present, under European law, everything is classified into three categories: people, capital and goods. Animals are classified as goods (or agricultural products), whether they are alive or dead. Consequently, under the Treaty of Rome, animals have the same moral status as ballpoint pens and dishwashers. They are not recognized as having any special ethical status because the EU is primarily a free-trade zone. Animals reared in Scotland can be transported to Italy or Spain. Welsh sheep are trucked to France for slaughter because there is a greater profit margin on Welsh lamb slaughtered there. Animals are at the mercy of currency fluctuations, speculators and farmers: the only way that this can change permanently is for the Treaty of Rome to be amended to reclassify them as sentient beings and not as commodities. This campaign is backed by all the main animal welfare groups.

The farming industry will attack this book as idealistic nonsense. I prefer to see it as part of the search for an ideal reality. Animals cannot fight to improve their own welfare so humans must fight for them. A resources section at the end of the book contains all you need to know to begin your fight to improve animal welfare across Europe. The battle to stop live exports showed the power of individuals. Welfare groups were occasionally offered seats around the table with the Government but were ignored. The people of Shoreham, Brightlingsea, Coventry and elsewhere pursued their own path through direct action. For this reason, the most effective way of bringing about change is through individual action.

PART ONE

Animal Machines

1

The Wealth of Species

There are two sides to farming. The first is the ad man's delusion, in which chickens scratch around in the dirt, pigs snuffle their way through piles of apples in an orchard whilst cows watch lazily and chew the cud: this is the image projected on egg boxes and ready-made meals. The second side is propelled by economics and the pursuit of profit.

Farming is led by the market and it is not possible to understand the position of animals on the farm without a cursory understanding of how the pursuit of profit drives the farmer. For the average farmer, animals are living machines to turn raw materials, grass, grains, drugs and water, into meat, eggs and dairy products. There is no romance. The purpose of animals is to produce food. In the West, the demand for food is broadly static: the types of food may vary from decade to decade but the quantity does not change significantly. Because demand is static the farmer is in vicious competition with others to provide and sell those raw foods. This imposes a great economic discipline. The farmer must either be one of the lowest cost producers, or have a unique product, or eventually go out of business.

In theory, the market's invisible hand should benefit the consumer because only the cheapest and most innovative producers stay in business. Over the years, the theory goes, the consumer benefits from better products at the same or lower prices as productivity climbs ever higher. Farmers should also benefit because the products they use are provided at the lowest price. Consumers also benefit because they can impose their views on the market and get a response, either a better product or a cheaper one. The consumer gets what they want, providing they can pay for it. At the moment, the consumer demands cheap meat and the farmer produces it. If the consumer demanded healthier or more welfare-friendly meat then, in theory, the farmer would produce that instead. However, when it comes to livestock farming there is an unwitting third party: the animals. They are sentient beings, capable of thought and emotion (see Part Three), but have no way of imposing their interests or demands on the market. They are trapped inside a system over which they have no collective power.

An unregulated market knows no bounds: slavery, for instance, should be allowed in an unregulated market as would prostitution, but we have laws that lay down minimum standards and impose a degree of morality on the market. Few laws impose minimum standards of morality on the farmer. A farmer cannot cause 'unnecessary suffering' but, in practice, that means precious little to the animals on the slab. Unnecessary suffering to the farmer means that which causes unnecessary loss of capital. It bears no relation to an animal's physical or mental state. Welfare standards have been set deliberately low so as to not interfere with the market but also to give the illusion of setting minimum standards. In practice, farmers are rarely charged with or convicted of causing unnecessary suffering because they have an implicit understanding with the Ministry of Agriculture, Fisheries and Food (MAFF), the Government department responsible for farming, who have no interest in interfering with the farmer. In essence, the MAFF does not want to impose the additional costs that a high standard of animal welfare would bring. It is a Ministry of Agriculture, not of Food and Animal Welfare.

Before the 1930s, farms were usually 'mixed': most grew grains, had a couple of dozen chickens and a few pigs for eggs and meat. In hilly areas the farmer may have kept sheep. The richer ones would also have had cows for milk, and their calves were reared for meat. Farming was low intensity and low impact. Small farmers and their animals lived in poverty: the animals' low productivity meant that they weren't worth much to the farmer so they were poorly treated.

After the Second World War, the Government encouraged farmers to produce more food for an increasingly affluent society. For the first time meat, eggs and dairy products all became freely available. The early beneficiaries were the animals: the farmer could afford to treat them better because it made economic sense to do so. They were fed nutritious foods and given adequate housing for the first time. They were pampered because they would grow faster and in the end produce more. After a few years, though, only the cows and the sheep remained free to roam out of doors. The pigs and chickens, with the farmer, have become ensnared in the race to maximize profit.

The more a farmer invests in the animals the harder they have to be worked to get a return on the investment. The economic logic is straightforward: for a farmer to make a profit, the meat, milk and eggs must be worth more than the expense of producing them. The cost of producing the goods is broken down into two parts: fixed and variable costs. Fixed costs are those things that do not change whether, for example, the farmer produces five or fifty pigs: buildings, loan repayments, wages and equipment all fall into this category. Variable costs change with the numbers of animals raised, and include food and stock replacement. Clearly, then, the farmer makes no profit until all fixed costs are covered; thereafter he or she is on a steeply rising slope of profit. The more animals reared under the umbrella of the fixed costs the more money will be made.

For example, if a farmer has one building for rearing pigs which costs £900 per year to run, each animal can be sold for £100 and the variable costs are £10 per pig then the farmer has to sell 10 animals to break even. If the farmer produces 20 pigs and sells them for £2,000, then he will make £900 profit because the fixed costs are the same and the variable costs amount to only £200. If he sells 40 pigs the profit would be £2,700. Clearly, there is a great incentive to maximize production by increasing the numbers of animals reared in the building. These basic economic facts also determine how hard an animal is worked. Where fixed costs are relatively low the farmer has little incentive to force the animals to work harder by, say, increasing meat production through feeding them high-energy food and making them grow faster.

It is more profitable to minimize input and effectively treat them as sentient beings by leaving them to their own devices. If, on the other hand, fixed costs are high, it makes economic sense to force them to work harder. The easiest way to maximize meat production is to pack in the animals as densely as possible and force them to grow as fast as possible. Quite simply, it makes economic sense to treat animals as productive units akin to machines.

Once one farmer had made the decision to house his animals indoors, the forces of economics further narrowed his options, but also forced his competitors to do the same or go out of business. The decision to house animals indoors made ruthless economic sense. Because most of a farmer's investment was fixed, in increasingly sophisticated, expensive buildings and equipment, the rationale was to maximize the investment by packing in the animals tightly and ensuring that the maximum number passed through the rearing unit each year. Animals were bred to grow as fast and as efficiently as possible. Broiler chickens, used for meat, now reach slaughter weight in just 42 days after hatching, twice as fast as 30 years ago. They also have huge fleshy breasts, which is the meat most consumers prefer. They suffer terribly because their legs cannot keep up with the weight of the rapidly growing body. As a result, nearly 200 million chickens suffer each year from chronic leg pain. The new, heated farm buildings also mean that less of an animal's energy is wasted in keeping warm so more is available for growth. Because they are confined in small units they expend less energy than they would if they could move around and play freely.

A First Step Forward?

There have been several attempts to reverse this trend and put a humane dimension back into farming. All have failed. One of the most significant came with the ground-breaking Brambell Report on intensive husbandry in 1965, which followed Ruth Harrison's exposé of factory farming in *Animal Machines* and pressure from the *Observer* newspaper. This Government committee concluded that all animals should at least have the freedom to 'stand up, lie down, turn around, groom themselves and stretch their limbs'. The recommendations became known as the Five Freedoms. The committee believed it had laid the foundations for a significant reduction in the suffering of farm animals. The Five Freedoms were subsequently revised in 1993, when they were updated and extended by the Farm Animal Welfare Council, another committee, to form a more comprehensive list of farm animals' basic requirements. Even though the Five Freedoms came from advisors to the Government, they are the nearest thing animals have to a bill of rights. If they were enshrined in law, and coupled with amendments to the Treaty of Rome to recognize that animals are sentient, they would form the first step to establishing the rights of animals in British and European law (see Part Three).

The Five Freedoms
   (1) Freedom from thirst, hunger and malnutrition: animals should have easy access to fresh, clean water and adequate, nutritious food.

   (2) Freedom from discomfort: animals should live in an environment suitable to their species, including adequate shelter and a comfortable rest area.

   (3) Freedom from pain, injury and disease: by prevention, rapid diagnosis and treatment.

   (4) Freedom to express normal behaviour: by the provision of sufficient space, proper facilities and company of their own kind.

   (5) Freedom from fear and distress: by ensuring that living conditions avoid mental suffering.

Animals denied the five freedoms suffer an array of behavioural problems, many of which are alarmingly similar to those occurring in humans under stress. In a satisfactory environment, where a creature has all it needs to survive including sufficient mental challenges, it will act to control how it feels and will not suffer any undue stress. If it lacks any of the basic freedoms and cannot constructively improve its own welfare then it will become frustrated and behave more like a deranged Vietnam veteran than a normal well-balanced creature.

There are four types of frustration behaviour seen in humans and animals. 'Displacement' behaviour is seen after an animal is aroused by a strong stimulus, such as food or sex, and then denied the opportunity to satisfy its desire. Humans and animals often react in the same way. After a family argument a human may storm off and clean the windows; an animal similarly frustrated may groom itself. Both are attempting to dissipate strong feelings by using up mental energy in a useful activity to take their minds off their frustration. 'Rebound' behaviour is noticed when a creature is prevented from behaving in a certain way; when that behaviour becomes possible again they devote an unusually long period of time to it. Consider the behaviour of young lovers, separated then reunited, or a starving dog provided with food. 'Stereotypic' behaviour is another way in which people and animals dissipate frustration: if creatures are confined to a barren environment with nothing to do they may invent ways of consuming their time; over the years their actions deviate further and further from the norm and develop into ceaseless purposeless activities. Caged tigers may walk endlessly around the perimeter fence; prisoners do the same in their cells. 'Learned helplessness' is another kind of deranged behaviour: animals that have been involved in experiments, where they have been denied basic needs like food or company, often lose responsiveness to, say, electric shocks or to hunger. The experimenters say they have 'learned helplessness' and call this an adaptive response. John Webster, Professor of Animal Husbandry at Bristol University, is more exact. He calls it 'learned hopelessness'. After years of violent abuse many battered wives 'learn' the same response.

All these behaviour types are seen in animals on factory farms where all live in artificial surroundings that are rarely suited to their species. Whether they are battery chickens in their cages or pigs in sow stalls, all experience the same mental anguish that would drive many humans to suicide – but factory-farmed animals do not have that option.

2

The Cow

Odd as it may seem, the cow is probably the most abused animal on the farm. Cows appear to be less touched by the drive towards agricultural intensification than any other animal. They seem to have plenty of room to move around, enough food and they spend a large part of the day chewing the cud and watching the world pass by. But this is an illusion. Although freedom to move around is an important part of an animal's life, it is by no means all that is required to make it happy and contented. Of the five freedoms, however, this is the only one granted to the cow – and it, too, is likely soon to be withdrawn in the drive to increase profit.

Beef Cattle

There are about 12 million cattle in Britain, of which around 2.7 million are used for milk production, the rest for breeding and beef. Of all farm animals, beef cattle are probably treated least inhumanely. Yet in the UK, only half the beef produced comes from animals reared in open fields and suckled by their mothers. The rest comes from calves reared apart from their mothers. Because milk is a valuable commodity calves are rarely allowed to drink it; instead they are fed on waste milk products from the EU's intervention stores. Then they are grown fast on intensive pastures and high-energy foodstuffs before being slaughtered at about eighteen months.

Beef animals are not selected solely for maximum size but for speed of growth and muscle production in specific areas or 'cuts'. Selective breeding has been carried to the extreme with the 'double muscled' Belgian Blue cattle. These animals do not have an extra set of muscles, as the name suggests, but they are enormous and provide huge cuts of flesh in the hindquarters. As a result, the calves often cannot pass through their mother's birth canals. The cows suffer repeated Caesarian sections preformed with only a local anaesthetic to dull the pain for a few hours. The resultant scarring leads to chronic pain. Some cows are forced to produce twins by the transplanting of two embryos into the uterus. This often leads to significant birth problems and frequently kills the cow unless the calves are removed by Caesarian.

The Milker

It is the milk cow that probably suffers the most from the drive towards agricultural efficiency. An average dairy cow will produce between 6,000 and 12,000 litres of milk per year or about 20–40 litres a day. The 'natural' level of milk production for a cow suckling her calf is no more than 1,000 litres per year. Milk is such a valuable product that cows are constantly in lactation. The pressure to produce milk forces the farmer to drive cows to their limit. To ensure that production never falters, cows are impregnated two to three months after giving birth and will produce a calf 9.5 months later. The cow is therefore simultaneously lactating and pregnant for 6–8 months and allowed to 'rest' for 6–8 weeks of the year. Even the resting period has an economic end: the animal is pregnant and the farmer knows she needs a little time to rebuild her reserves ready for the next heave – when she gives birth and begins lactating again.

The drive to increase milk production has taken a huge toll on the dairy cow. Because of the energy and nutrient requirements to produce all that milk, she can rarely withstand the strain for more than a few days. During her short life, her hunger is intense. Metabolic hunger, the frantic and insatiable desire for nutrients, puts the cow under great physical and psychological stress. Like all good mothers she gives her all for her offspring, which often means digging deep into her own body's nutrient reserves: calcium and other minerals are recruited from her bones, and fat reserves are mobilized. Farmers who push their cattle to the limit feed them high nutrient foods that may overload the digestive system but do not satisfy the craving to eat. According to John Webster the cow feels simultaneously tired, hungry and full-up. Her body becomes tired and worn out, and after six or seven years she is fit only for hamburgers.

Immediately after a calf is born, milk production is so sudden and so intense that nutrients are siphoned out of the cow's body and she suffers a huge metabolic load. The sudden scramble for nutrients within the body can lead to milk fever, caused by the sudden depletion of calcium reserves following the onset of lactation. About 5–8 per cent of cows succumb to the disease each year. If it is left untreated, the animal becomes severely weakened and may collapse and die. Many get 'grass staggers' from lack of magnesium. Nutrient depletion weakens the immune system, which becomes progressively unable to fight off disease. Brucellosis, which can lead to abortion and endometritis – inflation of the uterus – are caused both by lack of hygiene and a weakened immune system. Viral pneumonia and acute infection by salmonella bacteria are also common.

Automated milking damages the teats and lets in disease to the udder of which mastitis – generally caused by poor hygiene in milking cubicles – is the most common of the so-called production diseases. The infection may lead to depressed appetite, severe diarrhoea and dehydration. All in all, some pintas contain up to a million pus-forming cells per millilitre, and up to 25 per cent of British dairy herds fail to meet the new EU guidelines on pus levels in milk. Up to 20 litres of milk sloshing around in the udder at any one time – ten times more than the 'natural' amount – places great mechanical stress on the animal and may lead to lameness. Another common form of lameness is laminitis: Professor Webster says that the pain is similar 'to crushing all your fingers in the door then standing on your fingertips'. During the winter cows are frequently housed indoors, on floors slick with acidic faeces, which ensures that their feet progressively disintegrate. Generations of selective breeding have produced cows with a predisposition to lameness and others with slightly misshapen hips. This means that cows who inherit such disabilities cannot give birth easily, have slightly splayed legs and hooves that are easily damaged because they cannot walk properly.

In addition, dairy cows are frequently impregnated with semen from beef bulls resulting in calves too large for their birth canals.

Cheap Pet Food

Milk production also generates what amounts to a waste product: the calf, which is probably one of the most appealing sights on the farm. But the farmer, who is driven primarily by the profit motive and the need to maximize production while paring costs to the bone, has little interest in beauty. Every creature must earn its keep and most calves cannot do so. Three options are open to an animal not bred to replace its mother as a prime milk producer: it can be taken to market and sold for pet food – about 22,000 suffered this fate in 1994; it can be fattened for beef – 42 per cent of the 2.4 million steers, heifers and young bulls slaughtered in 1994 originated from a dairy herd; or it can be sold as veal.

Veal production is the most inhumane of all farm practices and relies on unremitting cruelty to produce the soft white flesh. Calves are separated from their dams when they are only a few days old and taken to market, often in appalling conditions. They have little value for the farmer so there is little incentive for him to ensure their welfare or survival: the only reason for their existence was to induce their mothers to produce milk and once lactation has started the calves are only a hindrance to their owner.

In the UK veal production is virtually non-existent because the crates used to produce it were banned, on humanitarian grounds, in 1990. But veal production in Europe is still very much alive and well and British calves are still exported there by the shipload. In 1994 about 500,000 British calves went to Continental veal producers. They are only a few days old when they are jammed into lorries under the not-so-quaint maxim of 'pile 'em high and sell 'em cheap'. An individual farmer may only take a few to market but, once there, they will join hundreds of others. A not untypical journey for a consignment of calves was exposed in 1995 when Albert Hall Farms Limited was convicted of 'transporting calves in a way likely to cause unnecessary suffering'. Early one morning some of the animals began their journey in the Isle of Wight. They went first to Wiltshire where they were sold, were then loaded up again before being transported to the Albert Hall Farms lairage near York, several hundred miles away. Without pause for the obligatory feeding, watering and resting stop, they were driven to Dover, at the other end of the country and another several hundred miles away. From there they went by ferry across the Channel, then by road to Southern France. Those calves travelled 1,100 miles over 37 hours without food, water or rest.

Albert Hall Farms were fined £12,000 but appeared to show little remorse or concern for the animals. Four months later they were back in court for a Judicial Review of the previous ruling. At that time animals could be transported for fifteen hours between feeding, watering and resting and the exporter claimed that each time the animals changed hands – for example, when they reached market – they effectively had a break because they had stopped moving. The judges ruled, however, that the point at issue was the journey experienced by the animals and not the journey of the paperwork.

Government Lies

In June 1995, after months of protests at ports and airports across the UK, the rules on live-animal transport were changed – for the worse. The story that caught the headlines was that transport times had been reduced from 15 hours to eight. But this was a classic example of government spin doctors at work: the real rules had been relaxed allowing animals to be transported for up to 28 hours without a break. Animals can now be transported continuously for up to 14 hours before they must be fed and watered on the trucks before another journey of 14 hours begins. The eight-hour figure applies to animals being carried in transporters without food and water. The exporters and MAFF are trying to work out how the new rules can be 'bent'. A week after they had been agreed a spokesman for MAFF said that he thought 'a bag of nuts and a trough of water' on board the truck may be all that is necessary for the exporters to comply. So, whereas previously animals could be transported for fifteen hours, they may now be transported for 28, providing they are thrown a bag of nuts and given a bucket of water *en route*. The net results of the new rules are that the exporters must 'upgrade' their trucks by adding food and water troughs, the Government can claim to have tackled the live-transport issue and the animals can continue to suffer.

Needless to say, the new rules were met with derision from all welfare groups, who described them as a 'whitewash'. The protests continued.

Real Veal

Once in Europe, the tiny week-old calves are kept in wooden slatted crates for the rest of their lives. After a few weeks' growth they cannot move: they are deliberately restricted because movement would allow them to produce muscle, which would spoil their tender white flesh. They are kept in semi-darkness, on an iron-deficient diet of a milk substitute. The lack of light and iron also helps to ensure that the meat stays white and anaemic. The crates are devoid of straw and other bedding, which might provide traces of iron or roughage. Growth is maximized by keeping the calves in hot, dry conditions without water to ensure that they drink the energy- and protein-rich reconstituted milk – real milk is too valuable to waste on them – fed to them twice a day through a latch at the front of the crate: it is probably the only time that the animals catch sight of their own kind. The lack of roughage in the diet ensures that stomach development is stunted. The calves become desperate for solid food: they lick the wooden floor in hunger and chew their own hair. As slaughter approaches they become increasingly sick, weak and anaemic. Eventually, after 12–16 weeks, they are slaughtered and guzzled down in gourmet restaurants.

Mad Cows and Englishmen

The dairy industry is now highly integrated: the waste products of one branch function as the raw material for another. Dairy calves are a waste product so they are converted into veal, a high-value product. Calves too feeble or sick for veal serve as a raw material for pet food. Burnt-out dairy cows become cheap cuts of meat or hamburgers. And until the BSE epidemic, sick or dying cows were converted into cattle food.

Rendering, or the conversion of waste meat, bones and offal into protein and fat for human and animal consumption, is a central pillar of the dairy industry and gave the world Bovine Spongiform Encephalopathy (BSE) also known as mad-cow disease. BSE tore through Britain's cows and in the late 1980s began to spread abroad. In 1993, at the height of the epidemic in cows, more than a thousand new cases of the disease were confirmed each week. By early 1996 there were strong indications that this deadly disease had spread to humans. Nobody knows how many cases of its human equivalent, Creutzfeldt-Jakob disease, will eventually arise.

The First Outbreak

Little is known about BSE. It began like a science-fiction B movie, quietly and unobtrusively on a small farm where one man knew that something was seriously amiss but couldn't work out what. In April 1985, Colin Whitaker, a vet, was called to a farm near Ashford in Kent by a farmer who said that one of his cows had developed a strange affliction: it had turned from a normal, docile animal into an aggressive and panicky creature that would charge around the farm-yard and periodically collapse in a fit. The vet's immediate conclusion was that the animal had developed a tumour so he put it out of its misery. Shortly afterwards he was summoned back to the farm to see several more cattle who were behaving in the same way, and samples were sent to MAFF's Central Veterinary Laboratory. After an exhaustive battery of tests, the Ministry concluded that the animals were suffering from a new cattle disease, and it was confirmed subsequently that they had discovered the world's first case of a spongiform, or brain-rotting disease, in cattle. In spongiform diseases the brain tissue gradually acquires tiny holes until it comes to resemble a sponge.

At that stage nobody knew the origin of the disease – indeed, even now, there is no definitive evidence but the best guess is that BSE evolved from scrapie, a spongiform disease of sheep. Once the scientists realized that scrapie had jumped the species barrier many began to worry: when this happens the disease may become a far more aggressive and effective parasite. Nobody can be certain how many species the disease-causing agent will be able to infect. Has this disease evolved a new trick that allows it to infect all breeds of cattle? All farm animals? Or even all mammals, including humans? The questions lurked at the back of the minds of scientists. It is highly unusual for a disease to jump from one species to another, and even more so from sheep to cows to man. But it was a chance that few cared to think about too deeply.

There's Only One Solution: Appoint a Committee

The disease continued to spread and hundreds of new cases were reported every week. Once the media had latched on to the epidemic, something had to be done. A committee was set up to investigate it and, in April 1988, Sir Richard Southwood was appointed its chair. At about the same time MAFF scientists thought that they had isolated the route of transmission from sheep to cattle. After analysing 200 cases of BSE, they identified a common factor in all cases: all the cattle had eaten food made from sheep infected with the brain-rotting disease scrapie. These sheep, together with slaughterhouse waste and the bodies of pigs, cattle, chickens, and sheep that had died from injury and other diseases, had been rendered down into cattle feed, even though cattle are herbivores.

Rendering capitalizes on the integration across the meat industry and is a direct result of the economic forces that drive agriculture. Like all efficient and highly integrated production systems, the waste from one part of the industry becomes the raw material for another. Waste from farms and slaughterhouses that could not be incorporated into processed meat products, like pies and hamburgers, was boiled up and the raw protein and fat incorporated into animal food. Until March 1996, all animal remains, bar a few organs believed to contain the BSE-causing agent, could be recycled into feed. And even the suspect organs had been a normal ingredient of animal feed until July 1988. The renderers, however, had been carrying on their trade for decades without any apparent problems of diseases jumping between species. So why did the disease only leap from sheep to cows in the early- to mid-eighties? Again the answer is unknown but it is a likely consequence of a change in the rendering production process, which occurred a few years before BSE reared its head.

Once again, agribusiness economics were to blame. Towards the end of the 1970s and in the early 1980s it became increasingly difficult to make a living as a renderer.

Cheap vegetable oils were displacing tallow, extracted from offal, in animal feed and profits were falling. The big players in the industry were forced into a hard decision: either they could intensify further, streamline their operations at significant cost, or go bankrupt. At the same time, MAFF relaxed the guidelines on rendering, which allowed those involved in it radically to alter their production process. Those with the capital resources streamlined their operations by introducing a new system to convert waste animals into animal fodder. The old process, a batch system, extracted the protein and fat by essentially boiling up all the waste at high temperatures until it could be separated into its components – just like a stew will separate after it has been cooked and allowed to stand. In the drive to cut costs the renderers adopted a continuous production system in which waste was continually fed into one end of the extraction system and the separate components came out at the other. It was as radical a change as the car industry underwent when it switched from building vehicles individually to the production line.

According to MAFF scientists, the new rendering process did not kill the scrapie-causing agent. Consequently, and probably for the first time, cattle came into contact with it and rapidly succumbed. The hypothesis is, of course, quite appealing for MAFF and the meat industry. It relies on there being a single source of infection, which could be cut off at a stroke. And that is what they tried to do. In July 1988, the Minister of Agriculture, John Gummer, announced that sheep and cattle offal and brains (specified bovine offal) could no longer be used in feedstuffs, but did not ban rendered-down flesh and bones. Several months later, 'specified bovine offal' was also removed from the human food chain. It took another eight years, though, during the second BSE crisis, before the Government finally outlawed the feeding of any waste flesh from cows and sheep to their own kind or to the other.

Trust Me I'm a Spin Doctor

In February 1989, the Southwood Committee reported. One of the key conclusions was that factory farming may have inherent risks. It concluded: 'Considering BSE and how this new disease has arisen has led us to question the wisdom of some of the intensive practices of modern husbandry because they risk exposing man to new zoonoses [diseases humans can catch from animals]', and on the risks of BSE posed to humans the report concluded: 'It is most unlikely that BSE will have any implications for human health. Nevertheless, if our assessments of these likelihoods are incorrect, the implications would be extremely serious . . . [But] with the very long incubation period of spongiform encephalopathies in humans, it may be a decade or more before complete reassurance can be given.'

At the time of the Southwood Committee's Report, MAFF and the Department of Health, who jointly announced the results, gave an upbeat assessment of BSE. They said: 'The report concludes that the risk of transmission of BSE to humans appears remote and it is therefore most unlikely that BSE will have any implications for human health.' As far as they were concerned we could consume British beef in safety; the public had no need to be alarmed.

Crucially, the Government did not accept one of the key recommendations of the Report. Southwood wanted BSE-riddled cows out of the human food chain as fast as possible, whatever the cost, to minimize the risk of the disease spreading to humans. He was worried that farmers would sell off their cows when they showed the first signs of BSE, to minimize profit loss and concluded that the best way to stop them entering the human food chain was to buy the cows at 75 per cent at least of their uninfected value. The Government offered only 50 per cent but was forced into a U-turn eighteen months later when it became clear that farmers were, indeed, selling their animals at the first sign of BSE. Inevitably, the majority of these animals were eaten by the general meat-eating public.

Over the following six or seven years stories cropped up periodically in the media about the possibility of BSE spreading to people and were generally dismissed as 'scares' by the Government and the meat industry, who repeated their favourite mantra: 'The public has no need to be alarmed.' They spoke continuously of 'reassuring the public' and 're-establishing public confidence' in the industry whenever one of the 'scares' erupted. They talked of everything but ways of eradicating the disease and preventing its spread to humans. They preferred instead to talk about the safety of British beef and to castigate the media for whipping up 'scare stories'. But the 'scares' did not go away.

There was, in fact, a series of them. In 1990 a BSE-type disease took hold in a herd of kudu at London Zoo. At about the same time, gemsbok and nyala both succumbed to a spongiform disease at Marwell Zoo, as did a cheetah. The gemsboks and nyalas are thought to have eaten scrapie-infected meat and the cheetah is believed to have eaten cattle meat that contained infective spinal material. Then came the monkeys. The Medical Research Council conducted a trial involving four marmoset monkeys to see if BSE could infect primates. Two were injected with material taken from scrapie-infected sheep, the others with tissue taken from BSE-infected cows. In December 1991 they announced their results: the two marmosets injected with material from scrapie-infected sheep died of a spongiform disease but the two injected with material taken from BSE-infected cows appeared alive and well. 'Beef given clean bill of health,' said the headline in the *Meat Trades Journal*. A few months later the headline changed: 'Primates are affected by BSE'. This followed a Medical Research Council announcement that the marmosets injected with material taken from BSE-afflicted cows had died of a spongiform disease. Was this the nail in the coffin for British beef? Not quite. The experiment had one flaw: it had been designed to see whether BSE could take root in primates. It could never prove that it can be transmitted under normal circumstances between animals or species. So the nagging doubt remained. Could it infect humans? MAFF continued trying not to answer the question in any meaningful sense. In November 1992 after a series of feeding tests on cuts of beef like silverside they concluded that there was no risk to humans.

Several independent scientists did not believe the reassurances. Dr Steven Dealler, a consultant microbiologist, says that 75 per cent of animal species exposed to the BSE-causing agent developed the disease. Therefore, he concluded, humans have a strong chance of susceptibility to it. His work, which he admits contains a high degree of uncertainty, concludes that if it spreads to humans the disease could kill anywhere between 10,000 and 10 million people. One of the main reasons for such a wide margin of error is that we know very little about spongiform diseases, which are radically different from all other diseases. All known life on this planet stores the information to reproduce in genes made from the chemicals DNA (deoxyribonucleic acid) or RNA (ribonucleic acid). These genes act as stores of information. The information is then turned into specific proteins, which act like tiny factories to make copies of the organism. The best guess is that BSE is caused by an agent that is radically different from all hitherto known life. It is thought to be a prion, an agent that consists of protein with no DNA or

RNA. The hypothesis is that somehow a prion does not store the information needed to make copies of itself as DNA or RNA and consists solely of protein, which means that much of our knowledge on combating disease may be useless against the spongiforms. It also means that the risk of BSE infecting humans cannot be quantified accurately. Several species suffer from spongiform diseases, which may not be related to each other; they are classified together because they have similar symptoms – progressive loss of brain function, manic dementia, coma and, finally, death. Nobody is certain, but they may be caused by the unique class of disease-causing agents known as prions, or maybe by the same variety of prion. These agents are thought to act like slowly replicating toxins and progressively destroy the brain. If ingested they build up and slowly make copies of themselves. If a low dose is eaten, the animal may die of old age or be slaughtered before the symptoms appear. After a higher dose, the symptoms may appear before death. A still higher dose may result in the appearance of symptoms when the animal is young. The more that is eaten, the sooner the animal dies. The appearance of symptoms is said to show dose-response relationship, which makes BSE a particular risk for children. They will have been exposed early to the disease and the prions will have built up to a dangerous level when the subject is perhaps in their twenties or thirties. This theory also explains how the disease spread from sheep to cattle and why it may pass to humans: the prions are tough and, because they are essentially protein, they were extracted and concentrated from the bodies of dead farm animals along with the rest of the creatures' proteins. Here is where the cost-cutting of the renderers came in: using the old batch system the prions were destroyed or inactivated; the new continuous system allowed them to pass through. In effect, they were concentrated and fed to their new hosts, built up and were concentrated again when those infected cows were themselves rendered down.

At each turn of the cycle the prions were concentrated and served up to their new hosts. Unfortunately, they were also being concentrated and served to humans. Estimates vary, but as little as one teaspoon of infected cattle feed may, in time, be enough to kill a cow. Nobody knows for certain whether this amount or, in fact, any quantity is lethal to humans.

The Second BSE Crisis

Dr Dealler and the other scientists who suggested that BSE may spread to humans were widely regarded as lunatics until 20 March 1996 when the paper walls carefully constructed by the Government and the meat industry collapsed. Stephen Dorrell, Secretary of State for Health, was forced to admit for the first time that BSE may spread to humans and cause Creutzfeldt-Jacob disease. CJD is rare in humans, about one case per million people per year, and is constant throughout much of the world. It is also predominantly a disease of the elderly. But scientists working for the National CJD Surveillance Unit noted that in 1994 the disease pattern had changed: it was beginning to occur in younger people and, by the end of 1995, ten cases had been reported. Not many, perhaps, but at the start of an epidemic there are only ever a handful of sufferers. Dr Rob Will, head of the National CJD Surveillance Unit, said: 'We are reporting a new phenomenon; a major cause for concern.'

His anxiety was reflected at the same time by the Spongiform Encephalopathy Advisory Committee (SEAC). Professor John Pattison, its chair, announced that 'We have now arising in 1994 and 1995, 10 cases of a variant of CJD that we have not seen before. The incubation period of spongiform encephalopathies is five to 15 years. This suggests something new is happening in the middle of 1995 that would have resulted from exposure in the middle to the late 1980s . . . [This] drives us inevitably to the conclusion that the most likely risk factor for these cases in the middle of the 1980s is exposure to BSE.'

After the announcement to a stunned House of Commons, Douglas Hogg, Minister of Agriculture, acted to reassure farmers and said that he did not believe that the findings would 'damage consumer confidence and thus the beef market'. The beef market promptly collapsed across Europe. The EU banned British beef and calf exports, followed swiftly by much of the rest of the world. Within two months more than 30,000 people had lost their jobs in the meat industry and the likely cost of the crisis was estimated at more than £2.4 billion over two years.

SEAC's findings sparked off Britain's biggest ever crisis with the EU since it joined the Community in 1973. The EU declared that until BSE had been eradicated from Britain, beef and calf exports were banned. The Government continued to insist that British beef was safe but agreed, nevertheless, to take all necessary measures to ensure that the epidemic was brought under control. The Continental consumer refused to be reassured as easily as the British had been.

The Government was forced to admit that its previous attempts to contain BSE had failed, and new guidelines stipulated that all cattle over 30 months old from BSE-infected herds and about 100,000 others thought to be most at risk of the disease were to be slaughtered, rendered and incinerated at the end of their useful lives. It also tightened the rules on rendering, and meat and bone-meal – believed to have caused the BSE epidemic – was finally banned from the animal food chain. All animal feed that may have contained rendered animal waste was recalled, and its possession became a criminal offence.

Will these measures work? According to Steven Dealler, they will remove the majority of infected material from the human food chain but will do little to eradicate the disease. If they had been adopted when the disease originally appeared, then by now BSE would have been long forgotten and there would have been no threat to public health. But that, of course, would have affected the profit margin of the meat industry. The Government and the industry preferred to keep the profits rolling in and to hope that the disease would decline spontaneously. The industry appears keen to convert virtually anything into animal food if there is money to be made. In Switzerland even human placentas and dead pets have been turned into animal feed.

As a further indication of the cavalier attitude of both Government and meat industry, the infected 'specified bovine offals' – which contained the disease-causing prions – were not destroyed but simply recycled into pig feed – the same mechanism that had led to BSE in the first place. This was only banned when the second BSE crisis occurred. It is now known that pigs, if injected with the infected material from cattle, can catch a BSE-type disease. MAFF seems reluctant to confirm or deny that pigs can catch the disease by eating infected meat: they are generally slaughtered and eaten before they can show symptoms of the disease. The BSE agent may, therefore, have found its way into human food through pigs as well as cattle.

BSE now seems to be spreading from cow to calf, which means that the disease is endemic to the dairy herd, but there are, as yet, no indications that it may spread through cows' milk. Meanwhile MAFF clings to the belief that cows are still becoming infected through contaminated feed, which shows that renderers and slaughtermen are still failing to obey the law and guard the health of consumers and farm animals.

If the disease is endemic, as appears likely, then the only solution is to destroy all infected herds. A worst-case scenario was depicted in a front-page headline in the *Independent* on 21 March 1996, the day after the crisis broke: 'We considered killing all 11 million cattle – the entire national herd.' That nightmare may still become reality. Millions of animals may have to be slaughtered at huge expense and the disease may spread to the beef consumer: the average Briton has eaten at least 80 meals made with beef from infected animals.

As yet there is no strong statistical indication of the likely death toll among humans, or even if there will be one, no strong evidence will be available until, at the earliest, late 1997 or 1998. The majority of the infected material was officially removed from the human food supply in the late eighties but some still leaked into cheap meat products, such as burgers and meat pies. An unknown number of people may have already taken a lethal dose of the BSE-causing agent. A slow disease may already be chewing its way through their nervous systems, and there is nothing they can do. Whether they ate the disease-causing agent as a result of government incompetence in delaying the removal of infected material from the human food supply, or meat industry greed in flouting the rules and allowing the material to 'leak' into the food chain, is academic.

Cows on Drugs – BST

MAFF may deny it but BSE is a 'production disease', the result of animals being worked so hard that they burn out and become repeatedly ill. Humans also get production diseases: typists suffer repetitive strain injury and miners contract silicosis. The production diseases of the farm are more severe and are a direct result of the system of agriculture that drives animals to the limits of their endurance. The hard-pressed dairy cow is likely to come under even greater stress in the next few years if the EU allows the use of a synthetic hormone, known as bovine somatotropin (BST), to boost milk production. The hormone, produced by a genetically engineered strain of bacteria, is virtually identical to naturally occurring bovine somatotropin, which regulates a cow's milk production. Its use will allow farmers even greater control over their animals' lactation – and of course this will boost profits.

A cow produces milk from each calving for about 305 days. After the birth of the calf, milk production rises steeply for the first 50 days and then slowly declines for the remaining 250. With a monthly injection of the synthetic hormone, BST, the farmer can keep up milk production in the final 150 days of lactation.

Organic Machines

The modern cow is a highly tuned and efficient machine, in many cases running at the limits of endurance. Most of a lactating cow's energy is now used for milk production and only a relatively small part for her own maintenance – to keep her body ticking over and for 'defensive reserves'. In the wild most of her energy would have been used in bodily maintenance and in replenishing fat and nutrient reserves. Selective breeding and a plentiful food supply has enabled the farmer to redistribute the cow's energy and milk production has been increased at the expense of energy used for bodily maintenance.

According to Dr Wolfgang Goldhorn,[1] former veterinarian director of the West German State Veterinary Service, however, the cow has always resisted attempts to decrease the energy and nutrients that she keeps in reserve. This 'emergency ration' has always remained stubbornly beyond the reach of the farmer who has not even been able to force her to access it even during the most intensive periods of milk production. According to Dr Goldhorn, BST will be the key to unlock the cow's emergency food ration, which will be used to boost milk supply when the cow would ordinarily be reducing its output. Ordinarily the cow bolsters its nutrient reserves after the prolonged period of the intense exertion required to produce milk. The reserves will be used to provide a more even flow of milk and will be put back instead during the short 'resting' period of 6–8 weeks following the end of lactation. Consequently, the cow will effectively be further weakened during milk production and will be stressed even more by the mad rush to replenish her reserves at the end of lactation and before the birth of the next calf.

Freedom No More

Dr Goldhorn says that BST will have a considerable negative impact on dairy-cow welfare. He says that milking cows will no longer graze in fields, which amounts to the abolition of the last of their 'Five Freedoms', because optimum milk production can only be achieved with concentrated feed and not with grass. Studies in West Germany indicate that only 50 per cent of cows respond to BST with higher milk production, so the cow is likely to undergo a further intensive bout of selective breeding with unpredictable consequences for animal welfare. He also claims that there will be an increased risk of metabolic disorders, such as ketosis, a disease that leads to depression and delirium, which will further reduce the cow's resistance to disease, as well as imbalances in key bodily salts, which can lead to infertility and paralysis.

There may also be implications for human health. Many bacteria and viruses naturally inhabit the cow and a constant war is fought between them and the animal. The change in metabolism through BST and the possible weakening of the cow's immune system may mean that the farmer will be forced to maintain the animal's health and production with antibiotics and other drugs. The residues from these drugs, according to Dr Goldhorn, may be passed on to the consumer of dairy products and meat. There may be another side effect: in calves, BST helps to regulate growth and unscrupulous farmers may be tempted to give BST to them to boost their growth rate and therefore increase profits. So how can the consumer reject milk taken from BST-treated cows? MAFF have made it difficult to do so. They have accepted the arguments put forward by the chemical companies and have refused to compel farmers to label milk from cows treated with the drug. 'Milk is milk is milk,' they say. The drug is being tested on several herds and the milk from those cows is mixed with the general milk pool. But for the consumer who wishes to avoid milk taken from BST-treated cows, there is one chink of hope: organically produced milk, certified by the Soil Association, is taken from cows reared without the use of BST and is likely to remain so even if the rest of the dairy industry embraces it.

The European BST Ban

The EU has banned the use of BST until at least the year 2000, but the United States allows it. Under World Trade Organizations (WTO) rules, which govern international trade, the markets for agricultural products are being prised open. No longer will trading blocs like the EU be allowed to exclude products from North America and the Third World. As a result, the full force of international free trade, which has greatly boosted the material prosperity of humankind, will sweep through agriculture. The principles governing trade, that the lowest-cost producer or the one that produces the most innovative product wins, will mark a new downward spiral for farm-animal welfare. The competition within Britain and Europe to produce the cheapest food has already turned animals into organic machines and once farmers have to face the full force of international competition they will have to fight even harder for their market share. The animals will be worked even harder and their productivity will be enhanced by all that the pharmaceutical companies and the genetic engineers have to offer. If BST is used on any significant scale outside Europe our farmers will be at a severe handicap in the international marketplace and also on their home turf. They will simply have to compete or go out of business.

But what will BST use mean for the European farmer and the consumer? It is impossible to say for certain but since the end of the Second World War small dairy farms have declined precipitously and there has been a corresponding dramatic rise in larger holdings. As farming became more complex and reliant on agrochemicals and drugs, economies of scale came more into play: it was not worth the farmer's effort to tend half a dozen cows. BST is likely to reinforce the tendency. The EU's current moratorium on its use exists principally because it fears that the small farmer will be driven out of business by the ever-larger milk factories.

In *Animal Welfare*, Professor John Webster sums up the BST issue thus: 'The risk that a higher proportion of cows will complete their short lives in a state of chronic exhaustion is equally real . . . if cows for commerce had the same rights as rats for research then this cost would have to be assessed against the 'benefit' to society of a drug which consumers in the rich world do not want, those in the poor cannot afford, a product which no dairy farmer actually needs and one which will drive some out of business. I rest this particular case.'

Free Trade?

The EU may be forced to allow the use of BST at the end of the ban because the ban itself is of dubious legality under WTO rules. It can be construed as a non-tariff barrier to trade and the EU could be forced therefore to open its markets to the drug after all. One possible solution is to label BST-treated milk and allow the public to decide not to buy it. Another is to reclassify animals under the Treaty of Rome as sentient beings. If animal welfare were part of Europe's constitution then a cast-iron defence could be made for retention of the BST ban and the WTO would be powerless to force a change in Europe's constitution, permitting BST to be injected into European cattle.

How Safe Is Your Liver?

The potential pitfalls of BST pale into insignificance when it comes to the illegal drugs farmers use to boost their animals' productivity. Animal drug running is a multi-million-pound industry, which is organized by the 'hormone mafia', operates across Europe and *is endangering your health*. Such is the value of this illegal trade that an MEP has been attacked because of his forthright opposition to the drugs, the homes of vets have been shot at and petrol-bombed, and in February 1994 a vet in the forefront of testing animals for illegal growth hormones was murdered.

The drugs are fed to animals to boost both their growth rate and their final slaughter weight, both of which have profit implications for the farmer. The most common illegal drug is clenbuterol – also known as angel dust. It is not a hormone but a beta-agonist related to the drugs taken by some bodybuilders and has a similar effect in animals. Cattle may put on as much as 17 pounds per day, as the drug encourages muscle growth at the expense of body fat. The cost incentives are appealing: estimates from Belgium suggest that some animals will grow in just six weeks from 800 up to 1,300 pounds in weight, which represents about an extra £300 profit per animal. Beef producers may sell hundreds of animals per year so the drug cocktails may bring in tens of thousands of pounds more. Some traders who 'finish' cattle – fatten them up and get them in good condition for slaughter – are reputed to earn £40,000 per month.

Angel Dust

Clenbuterol is dangerous to humans: in the six months between October 1992 and March 1993, meat containing clenbuterol residues killed two people in Spain and hospitalized a further 350. In France another person was killed and 800 taken to hospital with liver disorders. Throughout Europe the mild effects of a low level of exposure – palpitations, dizziness and tremors – are thought to have afflicted tens of thousands. Its use is widespread. A leaked draft report produced by the EU estimated that 80 per cent of Belgian, 60 per cent of Dutch and 25 per cent of British beef cattle are doped with illegal drugs. The use of the cocktails is now accepted by so many farmers that to produce the report the EU had to collect and analyse its own samples from cattle across the Continent. Normally they would rely on vets and scientists in each member state but local vets could be bribed all too easily or threatened to falsify results. Even after it had produced the report, the EU sat on it for nine months for fear of damaging the public's faith in the meat industry, eventually releasing a watered-down version, perhaps to protect farmers. But even the leaked draft may have underestimated the problem: farmers, like athletes in training, are learning fast how to mix drug cocktails so that the different chemicals mask each other and confuse the scientists. One senior EU official told the *Daily Telegraph* in 1993: 'I don't eat beef any more, I used to eat a steak a day. This stuff is not just clenbuterol – it's very dangerous. Some farmers don't know what they've got – they just chuck it in.'

Drug use, like much of the rest of factory farming, has its roots in post-war austerity, where the only aim was to maximize production and cut prices. The pharmaceutical industry was quick to spot a potential market: the first successful product was diethylstilbestrol (DES), which was injected into an animal's muscles and made it grow rapidly. But that, too, came at a price: it was a possible carcinogen and several countries banned its use. By the 1980s it had been suspected of inducing breast growth in baby boys and the early signs of puberty in Italian girls of less than a year old: the children's symptoms were linked to DES residues in certain meat-based baby foods. In 1988 a range of growth-promoting drugs was banned in the EU: only Britain voted against the resolution.

By 1994, meat exports from the United States plummeted from US$231 million in 1988 to $98 million and the US is now threatening to take action against the EU through the WTO because it is probably illegal to ban hormone-treated meat from entering Europe. And, needless to say, the pharmaceutical industry, sensing vast profits, wants the ban lifted.

The ban is controversial because it blocks the use of all growth-promoters, several of which have passed the licensing procedures in some European countries, as well as in the USA, Canada and Latin America. The EU's own scientific studies, commissioned before the ban was imposed in 1988, found that three 'natural' hormones, oestradiol beta-17, progesterone and testosterone, were not a threat to consumers, if used properly. In late 1995, the US case was reinforced when Codex, the international food standards body of the United Nations Food and Agriculture Organization and the World Health Organization (WHO), signified its approval of the five hormones used in the USA.

Drugs and Welfare

Potentially, the drugs can pose a serious hazard to animal welfare. Unscrupulous farmers could force their animals to be more productive by overdosing them with the hormones and the resulting rapid weight gain will stress joints and ligaments, hearts, circulatory systems and internal organs. Digestive systems will have to deal with increased amounts of high-energy foodstuffs, which means that the animals may have to endure constant discomfort, it not outright pain. It is also possible that these drugs may overstretch the body so much that the animals will simply keel over and die. Then they will probably be recycled into another agricultural by-product.

Slaughterhouse Five

After giving her all for milk, the dairy cow faces the steely knife of the slaughterman. Milk cows are burnt out and useless at 6–8 years old. Beef cattle are slaughtered at about 18 months and veal calves at 4–5 months. About 3.5 million cattle face the same fate every year.

English law requires animals to be 'slaughtered instantaneously or rendered instantaneously insensible to pain until death supervenes'. But the law fails to take into account the greatest welfare problem in the slaughtering process: fear. The animals know that they are going to die as soon as they are herded off the trucks and into the slaughterhouse. They can smell the warm blood of those who went before. They may not understand the concept of death but nature has programmed them to avoid at all costs being killed. And fear is a distinct problem for an animal consciously choking on its own blood.

Before reaching the slaughter bay they are driven off the trucks and mixed with unknown animals in holding pens. They may have had a long journey lasting many hours and will be tired, hungry, and either too hot or too cold. Fights may break out with other equally terrified creatures and many are injured. In the slaughter bay they are stunned with a captive bolt pistol. A gun-like instrument is place near the centre of the forehead and a retracting bolt fired into the brain. The animal is generally knocked unconscious by the blow to the skull and also by the extensive brain damage, which should occur. Percussion stunning may also be used, which differs in that the bolt does not enter the brain. Stunning an animal is a skilled job and if it is not done correctly the animal may remain conscious. Slaughtermen work on a piece basis so may be tempted to rush the job and force as many animals as they can through the system every day to maximize pay. The pistols are frequently poorly maintained and sometimes gum-up with liquefied brain tissue, blood and other fluids found in a slaughterhouse. The system will also fail if an animal's head is not correctly restrained to allow the bolt to be placed correctly on the skull. Neither is the process helped by the terrified thrashings of a 1,000-pound beef cow.

After it has been stunned, the animal is shackled, then raised off the ground where its throat is 'stuck', or slit; the blood is then pumped out by the still-beating heart. The severing of the main blood vessels should stop the bloodflow to the brain and kill the animal while it is unconscious. It will then be skinned, butchered and manufactured into a host of different products. Waste will be processed for lower-grade food. In the meat industry nothing is wasted.

Ritual Slaughter

Jewish and Muslim ritual slaughter is exempted from the need to stun animals before they are killed. Both religions require that only intact and healthy animals are killed for food. Stunning, they argue, mars the flesh and therefore breaks the religious rules. Cattle are slaughtered by having their throats cut while restrained in an upright pen, then bleed to death. Research has shown that they remain responsive to visual and tactile stimuli for up to 126 seconds after the cut is made. Whether this constitutes consciousness or not is open to question but there is no doubt that the animal is distressed for tens of seconds. If animals experience the same time-dilation effects as when seriously injured, as humans do, it may seem considerably longer, before they choke on their own blood and slip into unconsciousness.

In 1985 the Farm Animal Welfare Council said that religious slaughter causes suffering, argued that it was based on tradition rather than religious doctrine and recommended that it should be banned. The Humane Slaughter Association (HSA) has demonstrated to representatives of the Union of Muslim Organizations that, after stunning, animals are still alive at the time their throats are cut and that bleeding out is therefore more effective – both groups object to the presence of blood in their meat. The HSA has shown that percussion stunning does not cause injury to the animal and can, therefore, be used as part of religious slaughter. Many Muslims and Jews, however, have taken exception to the pressure to abandon religious slaughter and see it as a racially motivated attack on their culture and traditions. MAFF has not taken up the Farm Animal Welfare Council's recommendations and a growing movement is now applying pressure for ritual slaughter to be banned.

3

The Pig

When George Orwell wrote *Animal Farm* he cast each animal according to its intelligence. The horse served as the noble workman, able to push itself unthinkingly to the limits of endurance. The dog was the loyal and intelligent policeman and the pigs were cast as the controlling intelligentsia. Pigs are by far the brightest creatures on the farm – but they, like the cow and all other animals, are pushed to the limit of their endurance and their bodies exploited by humans for a variety of uses.

Pigs in the wild are woodland dwellers. They are inquisitive, social animals, who forage for nuts, seeds, roots and berries. Their curiosity, like that in man, means they have a great sense of fun and often spend hours alternately charging through undergrowth, playing and sleeping. Sows have a highly developed maternal instinct. All good attributes for a natural happy life, perhaps, but unfortunately for the pig, its roasted flesh tastes good to the human palate. The pig is probably more intelligent than the dog, yet while Westerners reel at the sight of dogs being slaughtered for food in the Far East, more than 15 million pigs are slaughtered in Britain each year. The pig has been turned from a happy-go-lucky farmyard scavenger into a meat machine.

Pig Breeding

The introduction of cheap and efficient farm machinery, coupled with a ready and expanding market, allowed the farmer to increase pig production. The most efficient way was to bring the animals indoors and house them in ever more confined and efficient buildings, which lowered unit feed and maintenance costs. Disease, and the attendant large losses of animals kept in close quarters, was kept at bay with vaccines and antibiotics. Today there is affordable pig-meat for all who want it.

A typical breeding sow is first mated when she is 6–8 months old and will produce 10–12 piglets 114 days later. The piglets are weaned after 2–4 weeks, rather than at the 12–14 weeks that would occur naturally. The sow is mated again 5–10 days later to repeat the cycle about every 140 days and will produce, on average, 23 weaned piglets per year. For most of her adult life she will be pregnant and mixing with others in the same condition. When she is feeding her piglets she will be confined in a farrowing crate to restrict her movement so that she cannot roll over and crush them. Once weaned, the piglets are grown and fattened for slaughter at 4–7 months. The sows are used solely for breeding pigs for slaughter and will themselves be turned into pork pies, sausages and low-grade foods after they are burnt out at 3–4 years old.

There are three main rearing systems for sows: outdoor arks, which are triangular sheds often located in fields; covered yards; and sow stalls, a type of high-density accommodation. All three provide the necessary food and water for the pigs' survival but vary markedly in their ability to supply the other basic needs of the animals. From an animal welfare viewpoint, the worst system is the sow stall, in which at the time of writing, about 40 per cent of all breeding pigs are kept. Essentially this is a metal cage so narrow that the animal cannot turn around. Some pigs are tethered in the cages with heavy chains or straps around the neck or body. The floors are concrete or slatted, may lack straw or other bedding and frequently cause the animals great discomfort. When first confined in the stalls, a sow often becomes distressed. One Ph.D. researcher from the University of Wageningen, the Netherlands,[2] working on sow behaviour in the stalls, describes their frantic struggles on being forced in: 'The sows threw themselves violently backwards, straining against the tether. Sows thrashed their heads about as they twisted and turned in their struggle to free themselves. Often loud screams were emitted and occasional individuals crashed bodily against the side boards of the tether stalls. This sometimes resulted in sows collapsing to the floor.'

In the stalls the animals often sustain a high rate of foot injuries, joint problems and cuts and bruises. It is not unusual for minor injuries to become infected, which affects the damaged joints, and for septic arthritis and chronic pain to follow. The bare concrete causes them to suffer from cold if they lie on it for too long. Even if they are housed in a warm atmosphere, as they generally are, the bare concrete constantly saps their body warmth.

The sows may adapt to the cold bare floors by adopting a new 'dog-sitting' resting position. This is not a problem in itself but it allows microbes from the floor to track upwards through the urinary tract and into the kidneys, which can be immensely painful. Many such physical problems can be avoided if the farmer provides straw for his animals to lie on. But straw brings its own problems for the farmer: it costs money and needs to be changed regularly or it encourages disease. Also, daily mucking out is far more time-consuming than hosing down a stall with disinfectant.

Death and Disease

Despite the use of drugs and disinfectants, intensification of pig production has created disease problems: viral pneumonia, meningitis, swine vesicular disease, blue ear disease and scours (diarrhoea) are just a few of the afflictions suffered by the animals, so to reduce their losses farmers resort constantly to doping their pigs with drug cocktails to manage the ever-present threat of an epidemic killing or weakening their stock and reducing the profit margin.

The animal in the bare stalls often suffer from chronic frustration and frequently spend much of the day chewing and gnawing at the bars of their cages. Their instincts, which drive them to grub about in woodland soils, explore their surroundings and play with their own kind, are completely frustrated which places an intolerable psychological load on them. Research has shown that pigs become frustrated in the units if they are given both food and a trough containing earth to root around in, the trough is very much their first choice. Only when they have satisfied their curiosity and frustration will they begin to eat.

The Farm Animal Welfare Council has criticized the stall and tether systems. In 1988 it said:

> Both stall and tether systems fail to meet certain welfare criteria to which we attach particular importance. As a result of their design the animals housed in them are prevented from exercising and displaying most natural behaviour patterns; in the wide range of systems seen by members there was little scope to reduce the continuing stress which can be caused by confinement in these systems . . . We recommend . . . that the Government should introduce legislation as a matter of urgency to prevent all further installations of these designs.[3]

The Government heeded that call: no new sow stalls or tethers can be installed in Britain and their use will be banned from 1999, but hundreds of thousands of animals are still kept in them and many, no doubt, will continue in them until the stroke of midnight on 31 December 1998. In Europe the tethers will be banned in 2005 – a comfortable distance away for the farmers – but no decision has been taken on the stalls, and in any case, meat from such animals will still be imported into Britain after the ban is implemented in the UK. If British meat eaters continue to eat pork from these systems it will amount to a classic case of exporting a welfare problem. And the British ban could, in theory, be overturned by the EU as an unfair trading restriction on British pig producers.

Yardies

Pigs are also kept in covered yards, which in most respects offer an improvement over the stalls and tethers, and significantly reduce the frustration they endure. In this system, the animals are housed in large, airy sheds and generally have a layer of straw on the floors to root around in. It is the layer of straw that makes all the difference for the pig: the animal's nature drives it to spend large parts of its day snuffling through leaves, roots and soil, to which straw provides an acceptable alternative. The simple act of providing the bedding also reduces another welfare problem – cold stress, which the animals encounter if they are forced to lie on concrete floors. But the covered yards have one major welfare drawback: the sows, being relatively aggressive creatures, often fight because they lack sufficient space. Aggression is diffused if a recessive pig has somewhere to run to, which, in a covered yard, it does not. As a result, some pigs are bullied and suffer severe bites from the more dominant animals. Fighting is often a problem at feeding time. The farmer has been able to resolve this issue by providing the animals with individual feeding stalls, which are effective but expensive. New computerized feeding stalls are also being used, which allow the pigs to eat once or twice a day. Initially these made the aggression worse and some pigs were attacked by others as they entered and left the stalls. But, according to Professor Webster in *Animal Welfare*, the most elegant and cheapest solution is to scatter feed pellets over the surface of the yard. This way, the pigs have the pleasure of foraging and feeding, aggression is reduced, because they are dispersed over a wide area, and apparently not one pellet is wasted. The only possible drawback is that rations cannot be individually tailored to each sow but most of the time this is not a problem.

Arks

Pigs reared in outdoor arks are probably the happiest of the lot. Outdoor arks, long, low, triangular shaped buildings, provide the necessary shelter and the animals can fulfil most of their natural drives because they live in open fields. They are well fed but can root around and find the occasional extra morsel. Being able to snuffle through the earth all day makes for a considerably happier pig. But there is, of course, a down-side: many farmers use nose rings to stop their pigs digging, which is even more frustrating for the animals than living in a stall. Pigs in arks may also suffer from heat stress and sunburn in summer and from cold in winter, but these problems can be reduced by siting the arks on well-drained land, with plenty of straw, in winter, and by providing mud wallows in the summer. As with all animal husbandry systems, however, the primary aim should be not to eliminate stress but to provide an avenue for the creatures to solve their own problems.

Farrowing Crates

After a sow gives birth she is transferred to a farrowing crate, designed for both commercial and honourable reasons, to prevent her rolling on her young and crushing them. The metal cage allows the sow to stand up and lie down but the piglets can reach their mother's teats and are able to feed. Farrowing crates cause intense frustration for the sows because they cannot fulfil their primal urge to build a nest for their young and tend them properly.

Recent research has also demonstrated that there is little advantage to the crates. The numbers of piglets killed by crushing is broadly similar to those crushed in the outside arks.

Pigs for Meat

After weaning, when the piglets are 14–28 days old, they are transferred to nursery accommodation. The accelerated weaning may pose grave risks for the piglets: the sudden change in diet may lead to food allergies, indigestion or just plain hunger. Their immune systems may be suppressed and consequently they are prone to gastrointestinal infections. These problems are exacerbated by the stress of being removed from their mothers and a warm environment containing bedding and placed in a cold harsh pen.

The pigs are reared in groups in small pens or metal cages arranged in tiers. The slatted or perforated floors, often without bedding, can cause injury to legs and feet. The environment is generally barren, overcrowded and poorly lit and the pigs often become bored and aggressive. Fighting and especially tailbiting may occur, with which the farmer tries to cope by docking tails and clipping away teeth. Anaesthetics are rarely used. Male piglets may also be castrated to avoid 'boar taint', a strong flavour in the meat of mature males.

After about six weeks the pigs are transferred to fattening houses, which are usually indoor enclosures with concrete or slatted floors and no bedding. Pigs have been selectively bred to maximize their growth rate and many animals are not able to support their own weight: at least 15 per cent are thought to suffer lameness as a result of rapid growth overcoming the capability of their legs to support them. After 4–7 months the animals are slaughtered, although a few, who show the most desirable traits, may be retained for breeding.

Professor Donald Broom, chair of the European Union's Scientific Veterinary Committee, says that increasingly large numbers of pigs have leg problems and that rearing animals with bodies that grow too fast 'is rather like a child who is nine years old in weight having to stand on legs of, say, a five-year-old'.[4] They also grow too quickly for their heart, lungs and circulatory systems. Professor Broom says that these problems can reach critical proportions during transport. The pigs can 'have substantial problems because their muscles have grown faster than their blood vessels . . . they can be physiologically affected by not being able to get enough oxygen into their muscles and so even a young animal can have a heart attack and even die'. Over the decades and centuries of selective breeding the pig's heart has shrunk to almost half of its natural size in comparison to its bodyweight.

According to one study, published in *Biology of Stress in Farm Animals: an Integrated Approach*,[5] the heart of a wild boar constitutes 0.38 per cent of body weight. In the domestic pig it is just 0.21 per cent. During the process of selectively breeding chunky, muscular animals, the damaging halothane gene has also proliferated throughout the pig population. It contributes to lean flesh but is also associated with extreme sensitivity to stress which, combined with a weak heart, can often lead to sudden death. Attempts are now being made to breed out this gene and reduce the incidence of porcine stress syndrome and sudden death.

Death and the Pig

Once the pigs have reached slaughter weight they are transported to an abattoir and killed. According to Professor Webster, 'The welfare of pigs at the point of slaughter is a cause for real concern.' First they are herded, often in groups, into a stunning room and the slaughterman passes among them, stunning each animal with electric tongs placed across the head. The device, which looks like stereo headphones, passes an electric current through the brain before the animal's throat is slit. According to one study published in October 1993 in *Meat Manufacturing and Marketing*, nearly 20 per cent of pigs were improperly stunned or showed signs of recovery before they bled to death.[6] The problem lies with the relative low voltage of 90–120 volts used in the interests of the operator's safety. The person doing the stunning has to wade through a room full of pigs and attend to each in turn. The voltage may be too low for some pigs, while others may start to regain consciousness before the last is stunned and the throat-slitting begins.

One solution is for the animals to be delivered to the stunning point on a conveyor belt and for a higher voltage to be used. Another is to lower them into a chamber filled with carbon dioxide gas in which the animals slip into unconsciousness and suffocate. Unfortunately, these animals appear to suffer more than they would with correctly performed electrical stunning but the process is being refined and improved. If a mixture of carbon dioxide and argon is

used the animals slip into unconsciousness without any obvious distress and suffocate. If they are removed from the
chamber before they die they reawaken naturally and show
no aversion to re-entering the chamber. During one experiment, recounted by Professor Webster, a pig became unconscious while munching an apple, paused mid-chew and upon
reawakening carried on eating as if nothing had happened.

Gaseous stunning and killing is unlikely to become widespread in the near future because it would require substantial re-investment by slaughterhouse owners and would be
more costly to use on a day-to-day basis. Once again, the
only long-term solution is to amend the Treaty of Rome to
reclassify animals as sentient beings rather than agricultural
products, which would mean that inhumane slaughtering
methods could be outlawed. This would create a level playing-
field on which all agricultural producers could compete and
would make a huge difference to the lives and deaths of animals across Europe. In the shorter term, the obvious solution
is to improve labelling so that all meat products are clearly
identifiable as originating from farms that practise welfare-
friendly husbandry and genuinely humane slaughter methods. But without consumer pressure on supermarkets, even
this small step is far in the distance.

4

The Sheep

'I was standing on the block the other day and some sheep were coming through and one came running up to me and licked my hands and I said to my husband, "Why is he doing that?" and he said, "You should know, you fed him on the bottle three years ago." They're quite wonderful, really, they've got tremendous memories. I can't bear to see a sheep suffering. They don't make a fuss at all, they're a gentle sort of animal, very underrated. And I wonder if it's all worth it, really. I ask myself, Have we got the right? That's my problem.'

Alice Pritchard, sheep farmer's wife, Trecastle, Powys.[7]

The sheep industry has also been sucked into the spiral of agricultural intensification, where many farmers go out of business, the rest become richer and the animals pay the true price. Sheep farming is a hard business. It is still carried out mainly in upland areas where the elements take their toll on both farmer and animal. It is still largely a low-input and low-output industry but things are changing fast. Advancing technology and more efficient husbandry, not to mention EU subsidies, helped the British national flock increase from 34 million to 44 million animals between 1982 and 1992. Britain is now the largest producer of sheep meat in the EU and is responsible for about 40 per cent of the total. The UK is the fifth largest sheep-meat exporter in the world.

Money for Nothing:
Subsidies and the Sheep Farmer

Animals are treated according to their economic value to their owners. Pets are treated far better than food animals because they have an emotional worth where food animals do not. Time and money is only invested in an animal if there is a return, whether emotional or financial. A ewe going for slaughter may be worth only £30 whereas a breeding ram may be worth hundreds if not thousands of pounds. Consequently, the ewe will be left on a cold wet hillside throughout the winter before being loaded onto a draughty truck and transported across the country, or even across Europe, with 600 others before slaughter. They have little economic value so no one will invest time and money in caring for them.

This economic reality imposed by the present system exerts a strong hold over the sheep-rearing industry. To try to mitigate the worst of these realities, for the farmer, that is, not the animals, sheep farming is bailed out to a massive degree by European subsidies. More than 40 per cent of a typical sheep farmer's income comes from subsidies – far more than the beef industry, where 13.3 per cent of income derives from the tax-payer. The money is paid for socio-economic reasons rather than to boost food production. Sheep farming is generally uneconomic in the uplands, and as no European nation wants to see the collapse of hill farming it is heavily supported by the taxpayer. The price of wool, apart from that from the most expensive breeds, barely covers the cost of shearing so the farmer makes most money from meat.

The 1992 rejigging of European subsidies has fundamentally altered the economic structure of sheep farming. Farmers are now paid not for the number of animals produced and the flock size but for the numbers of sheep on the farm. The incentive, therefore, is to stock the animals as densely as possible and to provide them with little care, which maximizes the subsidy and therefore the profit. Under the original system the incentive was to maximize the number of healthy animals that reached the market and, therefore, the animals were better cared for. The new system combines the worst aspect of agribusiness, where animals have no inherent worth, with the harsh economic realities of hill farming. If animals were regarded as sentient beings, then the EU subsidies would have to be either redirected to maintain the upland farming communities with due regard to the welfare of animals or ceased completely. If there were no subsidies for sheep farming, the price of lamb would have to rise for the farmer to continue raising sheep. If the animals were worth more, they would be treated better.

This economic reality forces farmers to push sheep into the same economic spiral that has ensnared other livestock producers. Ewes will naturally produce one or two lambs per year but are capable of producing three. To increase the profit margin on the flock, farmers try to increase the average number of lambs born per ewe per year by using hormone and drug cocktails to induce triplets or by forcing their animals to produce three 'crops' every two years rather than the normal two. Ewes may be given fertility drugs to increase the numbers of eggs at ovulation, which results in twins or triplets, and to ensure that all ewes in a flock come in season at the same time, thus giving birth within days or even hours of each other. The drugs allow them to be artificially inseminated, which is still relatively rare in Britain with only about 17,000 procedures carried out annually.

Under natural conditions the ewe will be receptive to the ram around November or December but this only produces one lamb crop per year. To fool the ewe into producing three crops every two years – one as early as December – farmers trick her into thinking that autumn is on the way by injecting her with the hormone melatonin (which regulates the animal's body clock). To make sure that all the flock gives birth together, a sponge containing progesterone, which is also used in contraceptive pills, is inserted into the ewes' vaginas. When it is removed twelve days later the sudden rush of oestrogen induces ovulation and the ewe is ready to be serviced by the ram.

Artificial insemination is gradually becoming more commonly used. In sheep this is a complex procedure. A new form of artificial insemination requires the ewe to be upended on a rack and semen directly injected into her uterus. In *Animal Welfare*, Professor Webster says it is a 'classic example of non-therapeutic surgery which carries no benefit at all to the animal and is designed entirely for commercial gain'.

He goes on, 'It is not, in my opinion, sufficient to justify this procedure by legislation to ensure that it is performed under veterinary supervision. Such legislation is directed more towards the welfare of the veterinary profession than that of the sheep.' he says. For the ram it may be an even more painful experience: an electric probe is inserted into the anus and a shock administered to the prostrate gland to make it ejaculate. Margaret Price, a veterinary assistant at a practice in Llandovrey, said her practice always uses an anaesthetic but many vets do not. She said: 'I have actually seen a ram off his feet and writhing in agony having had this done.'

Lamb Production

After five months' gestation, the lambs are born. Upland lambs which are not yet subject to significant intensive rearing, are generally born in the spring – but spring in the hills and mountains of the north is often vicious. About 22 million lambs are born in Britain each year and 4 million die, often of exposure, within days of birth.[8] Lowland lambs are generally better cared-for: the ewes are over-wintered in special housing and many are scanned using ultrasound to see if they are carrying twins or triplets so that the farmer can feed them accordingly. The lambs are born indoors, away from snap chills and biting winds. Lowland sheep-farmers aim to produce a high proportion of twins and triplets, but because the ewe has only two teats, a third lamb must be quickly found a foster mother. If she does not readily accept it, she may be tethered by a rope or held by the neck in an adapter box, which looks like a set of stocks, for four or five days until she does. Lambs can also be fed by hand but this is more time-consuming and therefore expensive for the farmer.

Mutilations

Within days of birth male lambs undergo two painful procedures: castration and tail docking. Castration produces plump lamb and so boosts the amount of meat produced per animal. It also eliminates unplanned and therefore unprofitable breeding, and reduces aggression. The lambs are normally castrated with a tight rubber ring clamped around the testicles and scrotum which cuts off the blood supply. After a few weeks the dead tissues shrivel and fall off. The Farm Animal Welfare Council says that 'There is no doubt that all methods of castration and tailing [docking] cause pain and distress.' Applied too high up, said an article in *Sheep Farmer* magazine, a castration ring 'can trap the urethra, causing urine retention and, ultimately, renal [kidney] failure'.[9] The shepherd can surgically castrate lambs up to three months old without an anaesthetic, which often amounts to cutting off the testicles with a knife. In 1994 the Farm Animal Welfare Council recommended that this practice be banned except when performed by a surgeon under anaesthetic. It also recommended that the rubber-ring method should be allowed for lambs up to six weeks old. It is presently only allowed for animals aged less than a week.

The consumer's current preference for lean meat is forcing many farmers to rethink the desirability of castration. Uncastrated lambs are leaner and fitter – just what many health-conscious consumers want. If the animals are due to be slaughtered in the autumn before they reach breeding age, the farmer has no need to castrate the males and will produce the lean flesh for which the consumer is willing to pay a premium. Many farmers, mainly in lowlands areas, are now capitalizing on this drive for supposedly healthier meat.

Both male and female lambs generally have their tails docked shortly after birth. This is also a painful procedure in which a tight rubber ring is clamped around the base of the tail cutting off the blood supply. Tail docking is used to help prevent a devastating and painful affliction known as blowfly strike: maggots hatch from eggs laid in the dirty wool surrounding an animal's tail and rear end and eat their way through its flesh. Tail docking is generally seen as a positive contribution to sheep welfare, but Andrew Tyler of Animal Aid says the incidence of blowfly strike could be greatly lessened without recourse to tail docking through better shepherding. In Australia, the sheep fare worse: to reduce the incidence of blowfly strike the folds of flesh surrounding the tail are sliced away, without anaesthetic, to produce a wool-free scar. It is an easier and cheaper operation than regular shearing.

Mad Sheep Disease

Even though sheep and lambs are reared less intensively than most other farm animals they are still subject to a wide array of diseases, mostly caused by neglect rather than as a direct result of being pushed to their productive limits as cows, pigs and hens too often are. But production diseases are beginning to become more common in Britain's flocks as sheep-rearing becomes increasingly intensive. The drive for multiple births is increasing the level of lamb and ewe mortality. Pregnancy toxaemia, or twin-lamb disease, caused by the uterus pressing on the ewe's digestive system, can restrict her food intake, which weakens the ewe and her lambs, and reduces her output of sufficient high-quality milk. Poor-quality milk leaves the lambs open to a range of opportunistic diseases, including a bacterial infection known as watery mouth or rattle belly. This is generally diagnosed by a 'splashing sound if the lamb is gently shaken'.[10] Other symptoms are distended stomach and incessant drooling. Many sheep suffer from foot rot, which often results in lameness. The increasing use of high density housing and pens is believed to be contributing to this problem.

Sheep scab is also a major problem. It is combated, together with blowflies, by sheep-dipping, using organophosphate pesticides. These compounds, which were discovered during the search for battlefield nerve gases, kill virtually everything in the animal's wool and on its skin and are highly toxic both to the farmer and the sheep. In October 1994 the *Sheep Farmer* warned shepherds and shepherdesses that 'uncontrolled nervous signs' can result from using the wrong concentration or even if the farmer or his animals should swallow some of the agent. The symptoms of organophosphate poisoning include 'excessive salivation and tears, frequent urination, vomiting, difficulty in breathing, muscle twitching developing to uncoordination, paralysis, collapse and death'. In 1985 twice-yearly sheep-dipping was made compulsory to try to stamp out sheep scab and blowflies but, following concern about the health effects on the farmer, it was made optional again in 1992. In addition, users of the sheep-dipping compounds must now obtain a competence certificate before they may do so.

Sheep may also contract scrapie, from which BSE is thought to have originated. The symptoms include teeth grinding and lip twitching. If the animals are startled they may fall into an epileptic fit. They suffer from intense itching and lose all co-ordination. Paralysis is swiftly followed by death. There are no reliable estimates of the incidence of scrapie in Britain because it is not a notifiable disease. As the British Veterinary Association said in a memorandum to the House of Commons: 'We can only guess at the incidence of the disease. That has been an omission.' Most animals with scrapie, which has an incubation period of eighteen months–5 years, are eaten – and have been for centuries with no known ill effects – before the first symptoms appear, so despite its link to BSE, scrapie is unlikely to spread to humans.

Gateways to Hell: Live Exports

'If they were Jews in those trucks would you still help them through?' asked an anti-live-export protester of a Kent police officer.

'If that was the law, yes,' he replied.

Sheep are frequently transported hundreds if not thousands of miles on journeys lasting several days before slaughter. It was calves destined for veal crates that aroused huge protests in ports and airports across Britain during 1994/5, but sheep suffered just as much. More than 2 million are exported from Britain every year because of the twisted economics of farming. The big spur to the live export trade came in 1980s when French farming co-operatives built a series of massive slaughterhouses whose capacity ensured that a vast throughput of animals was required to maintain profit margins. The smaller British slaughterhouses were forced to close and the more efficient and profitable French ones captured their share of the market. Within a few years of the new slaughterhouses opening, live-animal exports from Britain to France exploded. It became highly profitable for middlemen to buy British sheep and ship them to France for slaughter. Although the profit on individual sheep was small, often less than £5, the number of animals involved, and therefore the total profit, was huge.

Many sheep are transported in appalling conditions. Sheep are cheap and are treated accordingly. They are loaded on to trucks at the farm and taken to market. Here they are subjected to the stresses of loading, unloading and hours of waiting. They are packed in tiny stalls on floors wet with excrement and urine before being sold. If a sheep is lucky it will be crammed into a lorry with 600 others and transported for a few hours before slaughter. If unlucky, it is exported. In 1993 a not untypical journey was exposed when one of the largest sheep exporters was convicted of causing unnecessary suffering. Richard Otley complied with the normal, minimal regulations and obtained a certificate to say that his animals were fit to travel. Immediately afterwards the sheep were shorn so that more could be packed into the trucks. But virtually naked sheep, open-sided lorries and freezing cold December weather don't mix and trading-standards officers, who intercepted the animals, estimated that 20 per cent would have died before reaching their destination. Otley was fined £7,000, subsequently reduced to

£3,000. In August 1994, another 400 sheep – not belonging to Otley – were despatched from Dover bound for Holland. Three hundred arrived dead in Greece. Don Balfour, head of the RSPCA's special-operations unit, summed up the views of many: 'It is an awful example of what can go wrong on these long journeys with live animals. I question why it is necessary to subject animals to such journeys when there are perfectly adequate slaughterhouses in this country and refrigerated lorries to carry the meat abroad.' Richard Otley, however, compared live transport to a skiing trip: 'It's not in our interests to overcrowd lorries and cause cruelty. Is there any cruelty in sending fifty-four people skiing if they're all crammed into a coach first?' The animals, he says, are even able to sleep whereas their human counterparts cannot.

Lambs to the Slaughter

On arrival at a British slaughterhouse the sheep are herded into a holding bay. They often suffer because of the strange surroundings and the presence of animals from different flocks, which they find disturbing. Many are terrified by the smell of blood and the sounds of the slaughterhouse. They often panic.

First they are electrically stunned with a low 70–90 volts before their throats are slit. The wool on the animal's head may provide extra resistance to the electric current, but most evidence suggests that sheep require a lower voltage than pigs, particularly if wet electrodes are used: the damp reduces the insulating effect of the wool. However, in response to welfare concerns, Norway has banned the use of low voltage stunning. In the UK about a tenth of sheep are stunned with the captive bolt pistol, which fires a retracting bolt into the brain.

Lambs are slaughtered at various ages to ensure a constant supply of meat to the markets.

5

The Chicken

During the time it takes you to read this page 11,500 chickens will be slaughtered. More than 700 million are reared and killed each year for meat in Britain and they are by far the most systematically abused creatures on the factory farm. The chicken is highly specialized and profitable bird. Honed by decades of increasing agricultural intensification, it now comes in two forms: the laying hen, used for eggs; and the broiler, used for meat. The chicken industry is hailed by the agricultural community as their first and greatest triumph because the meat and eggs are affordable by all who want them.

At the end of the Second World War chicken was a rarity. The tender white flesh was a by-product of the egg industry, came mostly from unwanted male chicks and as a consequence was scarce and costly. But the agricultural industry was quick to see the economic benefits of confining birds indoors and selectively breeding them for ever-faster flesh production. The industry has always been a model for intensive farming and many of the lessons learnt by the chicken and egg producers have been copied by the rest of the meat trade.

The poultry industry, which includes turkey producers, is a model for the way in which the meat-production sector is likely to develop. As a result of public pressure some in the chicken industry are now beginning to de-intensify but as consumers are fast switching away from red to white meat intensive chicken-rearing units are still proliferating.

Broiler chickens are reared in flocks of about 30,000 birds and confined in large windowless sheds with automatic feeding, watering and ventilation. Turkeys are reared in similar conditions. Often the only contact the farmer has with the birds is when they are introduced to the sheds, when they are removed for slaughter, and when the scores of dead are removed each day. The sheds start off with a thick layer of woodshavings on the floor but after a few weeks this has been replaced by manure. The broilers are introduced to the sheds when they are a few days old and they grow so swiftly that after a few weeks it is not possible to see the floor through the carpet of chickens. MAFF recommends that each bird should have an area equivalent to about one and a half times the size of this book when it is opened but no maximum stocking density has been prescribed. Instead, it is up to the individual farmer to decide on the optimum, taking in all relevant factors such as mortality rates associated with increasing stocking density and greater profit margins associated with packing in as many birds as possible. MAFF recommendations are frequently exceeded, says the Farm Animal Welfare Council, which stresses that in the interests of bird welfare, the maximum stocking level 'should not be exceeded at any time during the growing period'. The Council has also called for a maximum stocking density to be enshrined in law, a recommendation upon which the Government has yet to act.

The sheer numbers of birds in the units precludes the farmer from giving them any individual attention. A modern broiler unit may have four sheds each containing 30–40,000 birds. One stockman may be responsible for up to

160,000 chickens. If he dedicates four hours each day to inspecting the flocks then each bird will receive less than a tenth of a second's attention. Peter Stevenson of Compassion in World Farming says that the 'broiler industry appears to have abandoned any attempt to take responsibility for the health and welfare of individual birds. Inevitably in such conditions a large number of birds become diseased or injured or even die without receiving any treatment.'

The sheds are poorly lit, with the equivalent of candle-light, about 10 lux, to discourage aggression. The lighting in a typical office would be 3–500 lux. In many broiler sheds the light levels are even poorer at 2–3 lux. The Farm Animal Welfare Council says such lighting is unacceptably poor and suggest it should be sufficient to allow each bird to see and be seen clearly. The lights are kept on for about 23 hours per day. The remaining hour allows the birds to become used to total darkness in case the lights fail – the last thing a chicken farmer wants is 30,000 panicking birds.

Short but Not Sweet

The life of a broiler is brief: about 42 days. They grow twice as fast today as they did 30 years ago but their legs and hearts do not. The phenomenal body growth severely compromises welfare. The accelerated rate has been achieved through intensive selective breeding, rich diets and growth-promoting drugs. Eventually the chicken outgrows its skeletal strength and begins to suffer painful bone and joint problems. For the last 10–15 days of its life 'there are severe abnormalities of bone development which we know to be painful and crippling,' says Professor Webster, and most leg disorders 'can be attributed to birds that have grown too heavy for their limbs and/or become so distorted in shape as to impose unnatural stresses on their joints. In other words, this abuse of the principles of good welfare has arisen as a direct consequence of breeding, feeding and housing meat birds for maximum lean tissue growth rate to the virtual exclusion of all criteria that define soundness or sustained fitness.'[11]

Research published in 1992 in the *Veterinary Record* suggested that 90 per cent of birds had detectable abnormalities in their walking ability.[12] In about 26 per cent of cases they were likely to have suffered chronic pain. Compassion in World Farming has extrapolated these results for the whole British flock and estimate that at least 180 million birds per year suffer chronic pain. Four per cent of birds, about 14 million per year, were incapable of sustained walking and could only move with the help of their wings or by crawling. More data presented in 1994 to the World Poultry Science Association suggests that infections of joints or bones are also rampant and 4 per cent of broilers are thought to suffer from them.[13] Compassion in World Farming claims that because many of these infections are deep-seated and likely to be missed by meat inspectors at the slaughterhouse, a significant number of birds with bacterial infections are entering the human food chain.

Heart and Lung Failure

The hearts and lungs of broilers are unable to keep up with their rapid body growth and many birds develop congestive heart failure, which causes fluid to pool in the abdomen. The Agricultural and Food Research Council estimates that every year this kill about 1 per cent of birds, about 7 million in all. The National Farmers' Union says that 'levels of mortality in modern broilers are higher because of a higher incidence of heart and circulatory disorders in birds bred for higher yield of breast meat'.[14]

Because the birds are generally in pain, many prefer to squat on the ground where the manure induces blisters in their chests and feet and often burns their hocks. These problems could be eliminated if they had space to move freely and had healthy legs. The way to reduce, if not eliminate, leg problems is to breed birds that grow more slowly.

Broilers used for breeding suffer just as much as those used for meat. Peter Stevenson, political and legal director of Compassion in World Farming, says that 'the broiler industry has in effect bred animals which are simply not viable, in that they are unable to survive into adulthood without succumbing to crippling leg problems or heart disease. In the main this does not matter to the industry as the vast majority of birds will be slaughtered well before reaching adulthood. But the industry is in a bind. Some of the birds must survive into adulthood – the breeder flock, those which are to produce the subsequent generations. These birds must not only survive, but remain sufficiently healthy to breed. With modern broilers this is impossible unless the growth rate can be slowed down.'

With its usual degree of elegance, the industry has solved the problem: breeding stock are fed a restricted diet to reduce their growth rate. A recent report published in *Animal Welfare* found that diet-restricted broilers eat only a quarter of the amount they would consume if given free access to food.[15] The researchers said that the birds are driven to eat constantly and, as a consequence of the restricted diet, develop deranged behaviour patterns, known as stereotypies, such as incessant pecking at non-food objects and excessive preening. As a result, they concluded, the birds are 'chronically hungry, frustrated and stressed'. Unusually for poultry, the first of the Five Freedoms – freedom from thirst, hunger and malnutrition – is contravened.

Harvest Time

About 2.5 million broiler chickens die while being 'harvested' from the sheds and transported to the slaughterhouse. According to a paper published in the *Veterinary Record* about half die of heart failure and another third from physical injuries. The most common trauma was femurs dislocated at the hip. These were generally associated with haemorrhaging and in about a third of cases the bone had been driven up into the abdomen. The injuries occurred mainly at 'harvesting' – during which teams of catchers grab the birds and carry them by one leg, four birds to a hand, to the waiting trucks. The injuries could be greatly reduced by carrying the birds by two legs but this would take longer and be more costly. In the trucks the birds are confined in plastic drawers, where more deaths and serious injuries occur: heads and necks are crushed when the drawers are closed.

Research by Professor Webster has shown that the birds' discomfort does not end when they are loaded on to the trucks. On the journey to the slaughterhouse they are likely to suffer from either heat or cold, sometimes both, which are major killers during transit. The motion of the vehicle causes discomfort: because the birds have been wrenched away from their steady-state environment and placed in an entirely different and constantly fluxing one, they are terrified.

A modern poultry slaughterhouse is highly efficient and mechanized. The birds are shackled to a moving line and lowered one by one into an electrically charged water tank, which renders them unconscious in the vast majority of cases. They pass on to a neck slitter, which mostly kills them. A slaughterman is usually standing by to despatch any birds that are still alive. Then they are lowered into a tank of scalding water, which loosens the feathers prior to plucking.

Happy Chickens?

As with all slaughtering processes, the level of suffering depends on how efficiently the killing is done. In poultry slaughter, there are welfare problems intrinsic to the system. Clearly a panic stricken bird does not relish being suspended upside down and lowered into a tank of electrically charged water. But the main problem arises when an injured chicken, perhaps with one or both legs broken, is shackled and carried upside down. The pain is probably intense and may be prolonged. As with pig slaughter, gas stunning is more humane: not only do the birds slip into unconsciousness before dying but they could even be killed in the packing crates, and thus be spared unloading and shackling. In larger factory farms, the birds could be gassed in the sheds – but this process is a long way from being adopted by the poultry industry.

Peter Bradnock, chief executive of the British Poultry Meat Federation, says there is no systematic cruelty in the poultry industry and that they 'maintain the highest welfare standards'.

'There is no such thing as factory farmed chicken – it is not possible to grow animals on a factory line. They are grown naturally and are kept warm, well fed, safe from predators, free to move around and are well looked after. Rather than being overcrowded, the birds, which are naturally flocking creatures, always have adequate space to move around. Indeed they have to be able to move to reach their food and water troughs.' Mr Bradnock says that the Federation's members comply with all specific and relevant UK legislation on the welfare of broiler hens. In the eyes of many, however, the problem is that the legislation is clearly inadequate.

Chicken and Egg

'The modern layer is, after all, only a very efficient converting machine, changing the raw material – feedingstuffs – into the finished product – the egg.'

Farmer and Stockbreeder 1982[16]

The joy in the life of a laying hen is almost on a par with that of a broiler. There are about 33 million laying hens in Britain, about 85 per cent of them reared in battery cages. The cages received their name from the way they were stacked up in the giant sheds used to house them: over the years the phrase 'battery of cages' became shortened to battery. The original battery hens, of *circa* 1950, were probably not too badly off in comparison with their distant daughters today. They were originally introduced, one to a cage, so that the production of individual layers could be monitored in a scientific manner; the concept was much in vogue in the 1950s. Those farmers wishing to steal a march on the opposition began to pack in the hens two to a cage, then three, so that now the common range is 4–6 layers per cage. Battery hens are protected by law in the EU and each bird should have 450 square centimetres – about three-quarters of the size of this book when it is opened out. Such a paltry amount of space leads to numerous psychological and physical problems for a species that evolved for tree living and scrabbling around in the earth for food. But to the farmer productivity per unit area is always paramount.

The battery hen is a good example of the duplicity in the way humankind treats its food and its pets. The Protection of Birds Act 1954 states: 'If any person keeps or confines any bird whatsoever in any cage or their receptacle which is not sufficient in height, length or breadth to permit the bird to stretch its wings freely, he shall be guilty of an offence against the Act and be liable to a special penalty.'[17] In its way, the Act was stumbling towards the Five Freedoms. Birds need space to behave as naturally as possible – one of the Five Freedoms. Naturally, they have an innate need to flap their wings, if only to stretch the muscles. However, there is a proviso within the Act: 'Provided that this subsection shall not apply to poultry.' The feelings and sentience of poultry and parrots may be at about the same level but the vested interests of the meat industry will clearly do their best to prevent that from being recognized in law.

Assault and Battery

The batteries are arranged in huge windowless sheds containing about 30,000 birds. Ventilation, cooling (there is rarely heating), feeding and watering are all automatically controlled. The bird's feed may contain processed feathers, the minced-up remains of the uneconomic male chicks and the bodies of females that died under the strain of fast growth. This 'recycling' of chicken meat is an exact parallel of the process that led to the BSE epidemic in cattle. The feed may also contain antibiotics, growth promoters and yolk colourants.

Antibiotics serve two purposes for the industry: they help to boost the growth rate of the birds for as yet undiscovered reasons; and they suppress disease. They are most commonly dispensed to birds used for meat. The close surroundings in the cages and broiler sheds are havens for pathogenic microbes and antibiotics in the birds' food or water prevents disease tearing through the flocks. This practice may have grave consequences for human health: one antibiotic commonly used, known as avoparcin, has been linked to resistance to the medically vital drug vancomysin, which is a 'last resort' antibiotic used to kill Staphylococcus aureus (MRSA). MRSA causes a nasty range of septic infections, including blood poisoning. If an antibiotic is used too frequently or incorrectly the microbes may develop resistance to it, and also to related drugs, which transfer to other species of microbes. The armoury of drugs that can fight human disease is being rapidly whittled away by microbes that are constantly developing resistance to them.

Yolk colourants are of vital importance to the industry: consumers prefer eggs with 'wholesome' golden yolks. Unfortunately for the farmer, these are only produced by birds allowed to scratch around in the dirt for grubs and roots where nature's own colourants reside. Yolks from factory-farmed birds are pale and anaemic. The farmer can duplicate the healthy-looking golden yolks using a range of colourants which are added directly to the chickenfeed. The ever-helpful additive manufacturers even produce a chart, just like paint-makers, so that the farmer can choose the exact shade of gold desired by the consumer.

The birds are taken from the breeding farms when they are 18–20 weeks old and put in the cages where they will produce an average of 300 eggs per year – staggeringly more than their wild ancestors, who managed 12–20 eggs. The birds are generally well provided with food and water – not to do so would reduce their productivity and the profit margin. They rarely suffer from the heat or the cold either: if the hens were too cold they would consume more food to keep warm, which would reduce their unit productivity. Even so, most sheds do not need to be heated – 30,000 bodies generate considerable heat – but the sheds do require cooling even in the depths of winter. This is achieved by controlling ventilation. As a result, during cold weather ventilation may be restricted and noxious gases like ammonia can build up. This is likely to be unpleasant for the birds but is unlikely to harm them seriously.

To further maximize production, the lights are left on for

about 17 hours per day to encourage the birds to lay. It fools them into believing that they are living through an eternal laying season.

Bored and Aggressive

The hens also suffer because the thin wire floors of the cages cut into the skin of their feet. Their claws often grow too long because they cannot wear them down. On a traditional farm, a chicken's feet are subjected to a great deal of wear and tear as it scratches around for food, which simply does not happen in a battery cage. In extreme cases the claws grow and encircle the wire of a cage, which results in the bird being literally rooted to the spot. The lack of opportunity to wander about and scratch ensures that a chicken's bones are relatively weak: research published in the *Veterinary Record* has shown that the tibia can be up to 41 per cent stronger in birds reared on a floor than those in a cage.[18]

One of the most common injuries in battery-farmed birds is feather pecking. The sheer frustration of living in the cages leads the hens into a form of aberrant feeding behaviour and they peck out each other's feathers which must be painful for the victims and dried blood can often be seen on their bald patches. It may also be a corruption of the 'pecking order', which allows birds to establish a hierarchy. Clearly this is a major problem for birds housed in sheds of 30,000 when their natural group size is 6–8. Feather pecking is more common in barren environments, such as battery cages, than in other systems, and, according to Michael Appleby from the Institute of Ecology and Resource Management at the University of Edinburgh, it is further increased if the birds are fed on food that can be eaten quickly. In natural conditions feeding would occupy up to 50 per cent of a chicken's time and in battery conditions their natural instincts are therefore rechannelled out of boredom into destructive behaviour. Feather pecking may progress to cannibalism, which, paradoxically, is less common in battery cages than in other systems, like a perchery, because the small group in one cage limits the number of others an aberrant bird can attack and also prevents other hens from mimicking their behaviour.

Beakless Birds

To reduce feather pecking and cannibalism farmers frequently slice off the birds' beaks with red-hot blades. Even this barbaric solution is a considerable advance on the older method, which consisted of burning them off with a blow-torch, which was developed in the 1940s in the USA. Debeaking is fast but painful for the birds. *Poultry Digest* reported on the care that must be taken during the process: 'An excessively hot blade causes blisters in the mouth. A cold or dull blade may cause the development of a fleshy bulb-like growth on the end of the mandible. Such growths are very sensitive.'[19]

Joseph Mauldin, a poultry scientist from the University of Georgia, says: 'There are many cases of burned nostrils and severe mutilations due to incorrect procedures, which unquestionably influence acute and chronic pain, feeding behaviour and production factors. I have evaluated beak trimming quality for private broiler companies and most are contented to achieve 70 per cent falling into properly trimmed categories . . . Replacement pullets have their beaks trimmed by crews who are paid for quality rather than quality of work.'[20]

A hen's beak is more than a dull growth of horny material. It has more in common with our finger-tips than with our nails. Normal hens use their beaks as an organ to explore their environment, and when they are debeaked their whole lived are affected. They avoid using their beaks for anything other than eating. Hens often develop the same type of hypersensitivity seen in humans following the amputation of a limb. M. Gentle, of the Agricultural and Food Research Council, reported in *World's Poultry Science Journal* that 'it is fair to say that we do not know how much discomfort or pain birds experience after beak trimming but in a caring society they should be given the benefit of the doubt. To prevent cannibalism and feather pecking of poultry, good husbandry is essential and in circumstances where light intensity cannot be controlled the only alternative is to attempt to breed birds which do not exhibit these damaging traits.'[21] MAFF recommends that debeaking should only be carried out as a last resort – but this advice is widely ignored. However, the poultry industry has taken note of consumers' concerns: the operation is now known as beak trimming.

Unnatural Behaviour

Perhaps the greatest abuse of the simple laying hen is the restriction of its natural behaviour patterns. All factory-farming systems are designed to maximize productivity – allowances for creatures to express their natural behaviour are not a consideration. A typical battery hen clearly does not have sufficient space to be 'able without difficulty to turn around, groom itself, get up, lie down and stretch its limbs', as recommended by Professor Rogers Brambell in 1965. The Brambell Committee was set up to study the animal welfare implications of factory farming and most of its recommendations have still not been met. For a bird that is constantly in lay, the stress of not being able to construct a nest to protect her eggs and the resulting young is considerable. The hens cannot scratch around in search of food and space restrictions preclude normal comfort behaviours such as wing-flapping, stretching and body shaking. The sheer boredom causes considerable psychological problems that cannot be resolved and are expressed as feather pecking, cannibalism and hysteria. Hens confined in cages show extreme fear of the few humans who enter battery sheds, while those in other systems, such as barns or in a free-range environment, show intense curiosity and will often gather around the farmer. In some cases the birds may become hysterical and fling themselves at the wires of their cages and flap their wings insanely, injuring themselves severely. If a human displayed such behaviour we would assume he had despaired of life and was trying commit suicide.

Poultry scientists have tried to reduce the incidence of hysteria by feeding the birds tranquillizers, trimming their claws and reducing colony size and the stocking density. But the only way to stop it completely is to provide them with nests and perches. But this, of course, would reduce the farmer's profit margin because the birds would need more space, and egg collection would be more difficult. Battery cages, therefore, remain the same.

The chickens stay in the cages for about a year before they reach the end of their economic lives when egg production begins to tail off. They are then turned into cheap products like chicken soup and pies. The poultry farmer will often try to extend the economic life of the birds by starving them of food and water while at the same time reducing the length of time the lights are switched on. This shocks the birds into restarting their egg-production cycle. This process, known as enforced moulting, is now illegal in the UK – but the ever-resourceful farmer has found a way round it.

After a year in the cages, the birds are often completely neurotic and will avoid unusual food for several days out of fear. So, all the farmer needs to do to induce moulting and bypass the law is to feed his hens something different and their neurosis will do the rest. After a few days the hens start to eat and the farmer saves on the rearing costs of a new batch of chickens.

Harvest Time Again

When the farmer can no longer make profit from the hen it is removed for slaughter. The life of a 'spent' hen is cheap. They are hardly worth 'harvesting'. They are generally wrenched out of their cages by handlers faced with tens of thousands of birds and little time to remove them. Several studies have suggested that each bird is liable to sustain at least one broken bone when being removed from its cage. Those birds whose claws have grown around the wires of the cages are likely to be horrifically injured when they are yanked free. They are then bundled into waiting transporters and taken to the slaughterhouse, where they are dispatched in the same way as broilers.

6

The Myth of Cruelty-free Meat, Milk and Eggs

There are alternatives to the factory-farming system but they cost money. The economics driving agriculture are no different from those driving the electronics industry or the stock market: the aim is always to maximize profit by optimizing production and minimizing losses. If a farmer cannot make a sufficient profit by treating the animals humanely then either they will be abused or the consumer will have to pay a welfare premium at the supermarket checkout. Most farmers choose to maximize production of their animals by using the factory-farming methods described earlier, but an increasing number are rearing their animals less intensively and passing the resulting costs on to consumers. On this issue, the power rests with consumers, who must choose either to stop eating flesh or to purchase more welfare-friendly varieties. The farmer must then respond to their collective purchasing power or go out of business.

Meat is now sold under a variety of labels, which hint that it has been produced from happy, healthy animals. It's best not to believe them. The meat industry employs top advertising and marketing people, who are aware that consumers are increasingly demanding meat produced from pampered healthy animals. They are responding to these demands not by improving the welfare of farm animals but by repackaging their flesh.

There is no system of animal rearing that is cruelty-free, and only organic meat *appears* to inflict a lower degree of suffering on farm creatures. In principle, organic meat production is more humane because the health and welfare of livestock is considered important to the farmer. But there are pitfalls. Organic produce certified by the Soil Association – look for their logo – is from farmers who are generally more concerned with farming than in making huge sums of money – but they still have to make a reasonable profit to survive in business. There are other certifications for organically produced meat, which guarantee higher welfare provisions than what are prevalent in factory farms, but the Soil Association's standards are, in my opinion, the highest.

'Cruelty-free' Beef, Pork, Lamb and Milk

At present there are only two genuine alternatives to factory-farmed meat and milk, and its variants, marketed under various 'welfare friendly' banners. The *Freedom Foods* scheme, which operates with the approval of the RSPCA, encourages farmers to improve their animals' welfare; in return they may sell their products under the RSPCA Freedom Foods banner. It is designed to improve the welfare of farm animals but the standards set appear not to be significantly different from those existing in ordinary factory farming as farmers in the scheme are still allowed to clip chickens' beaks, dock pigs' tails and use farrowing crates for pregnant sows. The RSPCA says it is planning to raise the standards demanded by the scheme as soon as a sufficient number of farmers adopt it, but since the launch in 1994 it has not significantly altered it in any way.

Organic farming is based loosely around the Five Freedoms

and also bans mutilations like tail docking and debeaking. The animals are fed only natural organic foods without antibiotics, growth promoters or hormones like BST, and cannot be given anything produced from rendered animal protein. The Soil Association banned rendered animal protein five years before MAFF did. They also ban the use of poultry feed made from rendered remains of other birds. By putting the needs of the animal first, the farmers do not have to rely on routine doping but medicines can still be used to help ease the suffering of sick animals and nurse them back to health. Calves from organic cows may not be exported for veal, to prevent them from ending their days in veal crates. As of writing, the trade in calves has been suspended following the BSE crisis, but it is likely that once Europe begins to relax the ban the veal calf trade will resume. Consequently, buying organic milk is also the only way to avoid inadvertently supporting the veal trade. Organically raised calves are also fed fresh milk, preferably from their own mothers, to safeguard their health.

'Cruelty-free' Chicken

Poultry and eggs are sold under a plethora of different welfare guises. Most do little to ease the plight of broilers and egg-laying hens.

Indoor extensive systems adopt a legally specified stocking density lower than in the current broiler units of 12 birds per square metre. To try to limit the problems associated with rapid growth, the earliest slaughter age is fixed at 56 days, which offers only a marginal improvement over the broiler units.

Free range offers a slight improvement and there are three variants from which to choose: free range, traditional free range and free range total freedom. Free range hens are reared in sheds similar to those used in the indoor extensive system but have access to the outside world. The minimum slaughter age is fixed at 56 days and the highest stocking density is 13 birds per square metre in the sheds and one per square metre outside. But growth is still too rapid for optimum health and the birds may still be debeaked. The stocking density is also too high and, as a result, many birds are prevented from going outside because the dominant birds drive the recessive ones back indoors.

Traditional free range offers a lower stocking density inside, at 12 birds per square metre, and outside, at one per two square metres, but again access is limited because of the aggressive birds. The biggest improvement is that the system allows the farmer to rear only slow-growing varieties of poultry, which must not be slaughtered before 81 days. Problems associated with ultra-fast growth are therefore virtually eliminated. *But* debeaking is still allowed.

In the *free range total freedom* system, the requirements are exactly the same as for traditional free range but with a major step forward: the birds are allowed to wander around outside as they wish. As an added bonus they are never debeaked but this has not been prohibited by law. The relatively small flock size and low stocking density in combination with a slow-growing – and less aggressive – variety of chicken ensures that the birds do not have to be debeaked.

Organic produce unusually does not indicate that birds have enjoyed the best welfare provisions because farmers taking this approach are permitted to use fast-growing varieties of chicken with all the attendant welfare problems: the space and housing requirements are broadly the same as the traditional free range system. For those who wish to continue to eat poultry the free range total freedom system is the most welfare-friendly of all the options.

'Cruelty-free' Eggs

The poultry industry uses several different rearing systems, in addition to battery units, each of which contributes a few per cent to the total UK production. All are less cruel than the battery cage but each has its own drawbacks.

The *deep litter* system is essentially a large enclosed barn with hens packed in, seven to the square metre. They can, at least, move around but there are no perches. The flock size is usually 5,000–10,000, which effectively prevents the birds from establishing a stable pecking order (about 80 birds is the maximum for that) and their numbers ensure that the birds are almost as badly off as if they were in battery cages. The cramped living conditions mean that they are frequently aggressive and the farmers often resort to debeaking.

In *barn* or *perchery* systems, at least half of the birds must be able to use a perch at any one time but the stocking density is very high at 25 birds per square metre. However, the birds are more able to move around because of the perches. Debeaking is allowed.

Free range offers a bigger improvement over batteries but there are still problems associated with it. Free Range egg production systems are based on either deep-litter barns or a perchery but the birds have access to a compound outside the building. They are debeaked and kept in flocks numbering thousands, which leads to aggression because they cannot establish a stable pecking order.

The *organic* – and the most welfare-friendly – system is based around small, movable huts with flocks of about 50 birds. The stocking density out of doors is about 1,000 birds per hectare. Organic allows the use of barn- or perchery-type systems but the relatively low stocking density, small flock size and mild-mannered varieties of laying hen ensure that aggression is minimized and debeaking is not required.

Unfortunately birds from all systems will be harvested and transported in approximately the same way, with the exception of organic hens. But once they've arrived at the slaughterhouse, even these birds are just warm meat to the slaughterman.

PART TWO

Genetic Engineering: Redesigning Animals

7

In the Beginning . . .

Life and death appeared to me ideal bounds, which I should first break through, and pour a torrent of light into our dark world. A new species would bless me as its creator and source; many happy and excellent natures would owe their being to me . . . Pursuing these reflections, I thought that if I could bestow animation upon lifeless matter, I might in the process of time (although I now find it impossible) renew life where death had apparently devoted the body to corruption . . . I collected bones from charnel-houses and disturbed, with profane fingers, the tremendous secrets of the human frame . . . The dissecting room and the slaughterhouse furnished many of my materials . . . It was a most beautiful season; never did the fields bestow a more beautiful harvest, or the vines yield a more luxuriant vintage: but my eyes were insensible to the charms of nature . . . With an anxiety that almost amounted to agony, I collected the instruments of life around me, that I might infuse a spark of being into the lifeless thing that lay at my feet. It was already one in the morning; the rain pattered dismally against the panes, and my candle was nearly burnt out, when, by the glimmer of the half-extinguished light, I saw the dull yellow eye of the creature open; it breathed hard, and a convulsive motion agitated its limbs.

Frankenstein, **Mary Shelley**

Within a few years pig-to-human heart transplants are likely to be routine. Pigs are being engineered with human genes to make them grow faster; sheep have been turned into living drug factories; and a new breed of mouse has been developed to suffer and die from cancer within weeks of birth. Genetic engineering is a potent tool and the technology is on the verge of spawning a whole new branch of agriculture. 'Molecular pharming' – the use of living animals as miniature pharmaceutical factories to produce new drugs in their blood or milk – is one of the hottest areas of research. Theoretically, scientists can produce animals capable of synthesizing almost any human protein. Some of these products are already undergoing clinical trials: Pharmaceutical Proteins, based in Edinburgh, have engineered sheep with a human blood-clotting factor gene to help haemophiliacs, and have also produced modified sheep that secrete into their milk alpha-antitrypsin, a valuable enzyme which can be used to treat emphysema.

Other companies are redesigning cows to produce 'nutraceutical' cocktails, which consist of part drug, part food suspended in the milk and are respectable cousins of the 'smart drugs' used to increase IQ and strength.

But the genetic engineering of animals cannot be seen in isolation from history. It is another step along the road first trodden millennia ago by nomadic herdsmen. When the first animals were domesticated about eleven thousand years ago, humankind chose the creatures most appropriate for its uses and animals were selected for their leather, fleece, milk and meat. Over the centuries they were moulded to suit humanity's purposes. In one sense genetic engineering is another step along that road. In another, it is a completely different, faster and more efficient one – the difference, say, between firearms and nuclear weapons – and for the first time the characteristics of one species can be transferred into another. Previously only the traits inherent to a creature could be either enhanced or discarded. New animal species could not be created.

Early domestication took place in the Middle East and Asia where the peoples tamed dogs, goats and sheep. All three were used initially as sources of meat, but the dogs graduated quickly to become guardians while the sheep and goats were useful sources of milk and wool. Pigs were domesticated at about the same time, while chickens, descendants of the Indian jungle fowl, were tamed as recently as four thousand years ago.

Cattle were first adopted in the Middle East and Asia some seven or eight thousand years ago. The temperate climate in the Middle East, especially across the flood plains of the Nile, Euphrates and Tigris, with their fertile soils, was ideal for agriculture and cattle raising. Over the millennia domesticated animals were improved little by breeding. Instead a form of natural selection was at work: the animals most adapted to humanity's ways were more likely to breed, and gradually became less wild and more tame. It was a random process, with only the subconscious wishes of the farmer guiding animal breeding.

Over time many varieties of sheep, cattle, chickens and pigs were developed but sea-change occurred in the early 1700s when Scotland began to produce a surplus of cattle. The spare animals were killed and the English, especially, developed a taste for their flesh. Farmers quickly realized the potential wealth to be made in meat and began to breed selectively from those animals that grew quickly and converted grass, hay and grains into flesh with maximum efficiency. The replacement of oxen with horses also meant that farmers had to use their cattle for something else.

The foundations of modern cattle breeding were laid in the eighteenth century. In the 1760s, Robert Bakewell, in England, demonstrated that farm animals could be improved for specific purposes: his relatively simple method of breeding only from animals with desired characteristics was revolutionary and his ideas were quickly copied. In cattle, animals were selected for ever greater milk production or for faster flesh growth. Beef and milk breeds were honed to new peaks of efficiency and began to be treated as much like machines as animals. It was the same story for other farm animals.

Pigs have been bred selectively to meet a variety of uses in this century alone. The hogs developed in the early nineteenth century were heavy, fat animals used for lard production, but as lard became less important in the 1920s due to the introduction of cheaper vegetable oils, leaner animals were produced. Today the consumer demands even leaner meat and pigs have been bred accordingly.

Sheep have also been intensively bred in this century to suit different palates and local environment – in New Zealand mainly for meat and in America for both meat and wool.

The breeding of all livestock has been scientific and records of all breeding lines monitored with the constant goal of maximizing production for each unit of input. Only the best animals that expressed the desired characteristics were bred from, and the progeny of each mating was carefully monitored to gauge the usefulness of each breeding animal. Little by little, from generation to generation, productivity increased.

8

Modern Animal Breeding

Artificial Insemination

The next main steps in animal breeding came with the development of artificial insemination (AI) and embryo transfer. Both techniques are used to enhance the speed of selective breeding. AI is the transfer of semen artificially from the male to the female and was first developed as a practical proposition just after the end of the First World War. The then Soviet Union was the first to use it in the 1920s. Before the Second World War, the West took it up and it quickly became central to the industrialization of agriculture. Many consider it the most important agricultural development of modern times.

The great advantage of AI is that it allows the transfer of 'superior genetic traits' from one male to thousands of off-spring in a short time rather than having to wait for the male to mate individually with each female. Semen can be frozen for many years without loss of potency, so the system's versatility means that the traits most desired in animal breeds across the world can be enhanced by the breeder.

Professor Christopher Polge, former research scientist at the Agricultural and Food Research Council in Cambridge, says that one of his most poignant memories is from a visit to an AI centre in India: 'Here the generally low-producing local cattle were inseminated with semen from bulls of much higher genetic merit, some of which was imported from abroad. In consequence it has been possible to more than double milk production in these areas within the space of a few years. This has not only improved human nutrition but has provided an important source of income for impoverished farmers.'[22] But the same process of enhancing the desired traits has an important drawback, says Professor Polge: 'In some countries, for example, indigenous breeds are becoming highly diluted or even replaced as semen from more productive and improved breeds is increasingly used for promoting higher production. It is important therefore to consider the potential detrimental effect that may result from a reduction of genetic diversity in our animal populations with the resultant need for conservation.'

That reduction in genetic diversity, for centuries the mother lode from which breeders have fashioned the animals we use for food, clothing and pleasure, is posing a major dilemma for breeders. Essentially, animals are being ever more finely tuned for maximum production – but the downside is that the traits for which breeders do not select may be lost and problem traits may be enhanced. For example, the productivity of laying hens has increased from about 250 to about 300 eggs per year in the last decade alone. But the birds have also become far more aggressive, an unwanted trait that has been magnified through the breeding process. Resistance to certain diseases may also have been lost along with other characteristics for which we have as yet no obvious need. These problems have always faced all breeders of all animals, but the dilemma is more acute with AI because it has enhanced the speed at which creatures can be bred and important traits lost.

In response, organizations such as the Rare Breeds Survival Trust in the UK are trying to maintain and enhance the genetic diversity of farm animals. The United Nations' Food and Agriculture Organization is doing the same internationally.

Impregnation

Across Europe 90 per cent of cows are impregnated using AI and the year-on-year increase in milk production in the best herds demonstrates how effective a breeding tool it is. The productivity of the milk cow increases by about 1 per cent per year, and in beef cattle desirable traits, such as leanness, can be bred into the population in just a few years. There are no welfare problems inherent in the extraction of semen, neither are there normally any problems associated with the artificial insemination of cows. The procedure, like its extraction, is relatively straightforward: the most unpleasant part is probably undertaken by the farmer who has to put his hand up the cow's rectum to manipulate the cervix into the correct position for the insemination gun to squirt the semen into the animal.

In pigs there are welfare problems and sheep can face a horrific ordeal. In sheep AI is a complex and invasive procedure, requiring the ewe to be upended on a rack and the semen directly injected into the uterus via an incision in the stomach. For the ram it may be even more painful. An electric probe is inserted into the anus and a shock administered to the prostate gland to make the animal ejaculate.

AI has reached a bizarre peak in turkeys: the modern bird has been bred for massive muscle development to produce lots of tender flesh and the most effective way of doing this is to select for larger breast muscles. This has resulted in birds that are too heavy to mate: the only way they can reproduce is artificially. Male breeding turkeys are 'milked' two or three times a week by holding the bird on a stool and pressing two or three times on the abdomen, which induces the bird to ejaculate. Collecting semen may cause pain in the bird as it often results in haemorrhages in its reproductive system. Interestingly, the Report of the Committee to Consider the Ethical Implications of Emerging Technologies in the Breeding of Farm Animals, an advisory body working for MAFF, heavily criticized AI in poultry: ' . . . the breeding of birds who are physically incapable of engaging in behaviour which is natural to them is fundamentally objectionable'.

Embryo Transfer

Embryo transfer is an even more powerful technique than AI. An embryo is fertilized within an animal expressing 'superior' traits and allowed to develop for about a week or so before being transferred to an 'inferior' creature. The surrogate mother therefore produces offspring with which she has no genetic relationship, and the technique allows a whole herd of 'inferior' animals to give birth to a highly productive one in a single generation.

Although AI is the workhorse of animal and especially cattle breeding, ET is far more powerful. Using AI as the basis for intense selective breeding, incremental increases in production can be made during each generation. It is powerful but its full impact still relies on nature, which can be unpredictable, and it may take several generations to produce a top-quality and highly productive herd.

Multiple Ovulation and Embryo Transfer (MOET) allows the breeder, using a cocktail of drugs and hormones, to produce a number of eggs which are then fertilized. The procedure relies on a nucleus herd of animals from which all embryos are produced. The performance of dams, sires and progeny is closely monitored so that the required characteristics in a breed can be rapidly enhanced. The technique can be used for year-on-year improvements in productive capacity or for generating a new breed or strain, for, say, leaner beef, in a few short generations. The technique is particularly useful for enhancing the traits required for animals used in developing countries.

But the power to transform a herd in one generation is a double-edged sword: the resulting animal will generally be far more closely related genetically than those they replace, which may in turn reduce the ability of the animals to fight off transmissible diseases. They may also have the same predispositions to other diseases, such as susceptibility to foot or joint damage. But, more importantly, genetic diversity will be lost. These problems, however, are rarely at the forefront of a farmer's mind, when he or she is constantly battling to be the most cost-effective producer.

We may also be seeing the first major problem of the narrowing of the genetic base in cattle produced by these techniques in the rapid spread of BSE. It is known that the spread of spongiform diseases is strongly genetically related, because some breeds of sheep do not suffer from scrapie and some races of humans have a low incidence of Creutzfeldt-Jakob disease.

Multiple Ovulation and Embryo Transfer (MOET)

ET technology is advancing apace. It is still used mainly in cattle, with about 350,000 procedures performed per year world-wide. At the moment, a mixture of hormones is used to induce 'super-ovulation' – the rapid and frequent release of eggs for MOET – but this method may be replaced by a new technique, being developed in Canada, which uses ultrasound – similar to that used in baby scans but far more powerful – to punch a hole in the side of the animal's ovary and release an egg from the follicle in which it develops. The aim of the technique, according to the researchers, is to 'aspirate eggs daily from top donor cows for *in vitro* fertilization'. Once released and fertilized the eggs are allowed to develop in the uterus for a week before they are flushed out as embryos, with a rubber tube inserted through the cervix.

It is clearly a complex and delicate procedure and one with great scope for error. Like all complex procedures, practice is required. George Seidel, in *Hoard's Dairyman*, said in 1989: 'About 50 to 100 recovery attempts are required to learn to deal with the various situations that arise . . . very rarely a donor can be damaged permanently. So this is a technique which requires great skill, the learning of which may cause considerable suffering to cows.'

According to Professor Webster, MOET should be reserved ideally for rapid enhancement of cattle breeds rather than as a routine procedure on the average dairy or beef farm. He says: 'My expectation, rather than my moral wish, is that MOET and related procedures will only prove to be cost-effective when used to promote rapid genetic improvement . . . My other expectation is that many farmers will continue to be seduced by MOET salesmen and their veterinary colleagues into buying "services" that will do neither them nor their cows any good.'

Advancing the Art

For salesmen and vets it is another way to capitalize on high-tech agriculture. The more the animals are denied their rights and the farmer disenfranchised, the more money can be made by service providers, who are helping to swell Europe's food stocks at the expense of the taxpayer and are continuing to advance their art. A new method is being developed by Scottish Beef Developments, with the aim of using eggs extracted from the ovaries of slaughtered heifers which are then fertilized *in vitro*. Researchers in Canada have developed a technique to remove the ovaries of new-born calves – one is taken from each animal – which provides an abundant supply of eggs. Eggs have also been used from aborted foetuses.

The idea is to use the technique to implant beef-producing calf embryos into dairy cattle. On the surface it appears attractive. Instead of producing less profitable dairy calves why not implant higher-value beef embryos instead? As ever, there is a welfare price to be paid and the animals are picking up the tab. The beef calves are fatter and meatier than the dairy cow would naturally produce and so the number of difficult and prolonged births is increasing. For the beef cow the problems are even more acute: her value lies in her flesh and that of her offspring, so farmers are prepared to risk the death of their cows by implanting embryos that will produce calves too big for the cows' birth canals. There is also a drive towards producing twins, which places a great physiological burden on a cow because she is designed to produce only a single calf. But if she gets into difficulties during calving she can always be slaughtered shortly afterwards with no major loss of profit and her orphaned offspring reared by hand. With dairy cows the farmer has to be careful that a difficult birth does not reduce milk production. The net result is that an increasing number of beef cows have difficult or fatal births. Many others are dying shortly afterwards.

MOET is also being adapted for use in sheep and goats where the procedure requires surgery because of the difficulty of navigating into the uterus. Essentially, an incision is made into the animal's abdominal wall and the embryos injected. There are obvious welfare problems associated with this and, like all surgical techniques, a chance that the operation will go wrong or infection set in. Luckily, for the animals, it is a costly procedure and therefore not common. It is used even less in pigs because they are such prolific, well-honed animals and easily bred from artificial insemination.

Sex and Cloning

Selecting the sex of offspring is also likely to increase in the future. The advantages to the cattle industry, in particular, are immense. The technique would allow the farmer to produce only bull calves, to be used for beef production, or heifers, to be used as milkers. Farmers will also be able to optimize the ratio of the sexes to suit their own needs. At present, sexing embryos is difficult and expensive but that is likely to change, and the possibility of 'sexing' sperm is also being explored. Sperm do not have a sex but they contain the genetic potential to produce either a male or female embryo. Once viable, sex selection could be a great money spinner for the breeding industry and the farmer. It remains to be seen what effect sex selection will have on farm animals.

If an embryo is split at an early stage of development, when it contains only tens of cells, then genetically identical embryos or clones are produced. This occasionally happens naturally, for example in identical twins, but animal breeders would love to be able endlessly to multiply embryos with valuable traits to reduce the time taken in bringing new or modified breeds to market. Cloning of individual embryos is already used in the ET industry but the great step forward will come when the nuclei from individual cells in an embryo can be transferred to an egg cell and allowed to develop into an implantable embryo. The technique is a long way from being an economic proposition and, at present only 20–25 per cent of embryos develop into viable animals. If it can be perfected, though, the potential for animal breeders is immeasurable.

In principle there should be no welfare problems associated with cloning but the reality in the test-tube is somewhat different. Recent work has been a disaster for the animals concerned: the calves, which normally have a birthweight of about 80 pounds, sometimes developed to 150 pounds and had to be delivered by Caesarean section. The Milk Marketing Board, now Milk Marque, says that there are advantages to cloning as breeders 'are more likely to get a uniform product'. But it admits: 'Any problems involved along the way, such as large calves, are part of the research.'

9

Designer Creation:
the Future of Animal Exploitation

The existing animal-breeding techniques described so far are powerful and allow breeders to fashion and hone creatures to maximize their productivity. But they are slow, cumbersome and give nature too much leeway. Genetic engineering is changing all that. In principle, humanity is on the verge of creating new species and radically re-engineering the existing ones virtually as the scientist sees fit. Breeders will soon be capable of creating animals to fit the requirements of farmers and drug companies with great precision. Animals could be tailored for different tasks: need a pig to grow faster, or a tougher, more resilient sheep to graze on the edge of the Arctic Circle and whose flesh tastes like beef? No problem. Genetic engineering is one of humankind's greatest technologies but poses great dangers for animals on the factory farm. Lacking rights, they are at the mercy of breeders and drug companies, and society, lacking strong religious and moral convictions, may allow the rest of creation to be, more than ever, humanity's victim.

The Start of It all

In 1953, James Watson and Francis Crick discovered the structure of a molecule called deoxyribonucleic acid or

DNA. This molecule, the central pillar of life, is used by each cell to store in its nucleus the information necessary to reproduce. Units (akin to books) of this information are called genes, which carry all the information necessary to make a protein. The proteins act like miniature factories and perform a specific task and therefore define the characteristics of an organism: for example, there are genes for eye-colour. Everything an organism's cells do is controlled by one gene or a combination of several. Genes are physically arranged on chromosomes, which are analogous to library shelves. Copies of all these genetic 'shelves' are housed in the nucleus of each cell. The nucleus is, essentially, a genetic library.

Watson and Crick's discovery revolutionized biology because it unlocked how a cell stores information. In principle, this cellular data could then be altered and transferred between organisms: the characteristics of one organism could be transferred to another. But genetic engineering – the re-engineering of life – was tantalizingly out of reach until about twenty-five years ago when the 'restriction enzymes' were discovered. These enzymes recognize and cut through sections of DNA and allow the engineer to snip out genes and transfer them somewhere else – to another organism or even to a different species of organism. About ten years ago another advance allowed genetic engineers to produce billions of copies of virtually any gene they wanted. These technologies allow humanity to transfer any gene (known as a transgene) to any organism with relative ease. Genes that help one animal to resist a disease can be transferred to another. Genes that code for important human hormones or proteins can be transferred to an animal, which can then produce it in abundance at a knock-down price. New pharmaceuticals – hence 'molecular pharming' – can also be developed and produced in abundance by an animal. The possibilities of 'transgenics' – the transfer of genes between animal species – are almost endless but so are the possibilities of abuse and disaster for the animal kingdom.

Hits and Misses

Genetic engineers invariably work in the dark and virtually nothing is known about how the genes integrate into chromosomes. The site appears random and often multiple copies are inserted in the same or in many different chromosomes. The nuclei of transgenic animals can easily become littered with the gene that the scientists are trying to get the creature to express. Consequently, each transgenic animal is unique and may express entirely different characteristics. Because of this lack of control, mutants may be produced: the desired stretch of DNA can easily integrate anywhere, even in the middle of a useful gene, and this mutation may not rear its head for several generations. When it does, however, it can be disastrous for the animal concerned. It is also extremely difficult to control how a gene is expressed once it is inside an animal. Frequently a gene may only be needed at certain stages of development and in specific tissues and, with few exceptions, all cells contain all the genetic information needed to make a whole organism. The means by which genes are 'switched' on and off is, in many cases, completely unknown. Precise control is required to produce and maintain a complex animal. If a new gene is inserted there is frequently no way of controlling its expression and the engineers are generally forced to rely on luck. Clearly, in such cases, the animal's luck ran out when it entered the laboratory.

Because of the 'wastage', companies working with the transgenic animals would like to recoup some of their costs by selling them for meat. In Australia, this has already taken place.

Dr Tim O'Brien, of Compassion in World Farming, says: 'Of the 50,000–100,000 genes in farm animals, we know the identity and function of only 1–2 per cent. Making modifications to this genome is like playing with a chemistry set which has had all the labels removed. Except that in the case of gene transfer, the experimental materials are living, sentient creatures, capable of feeling the pain that is caused when the experiments inevitably go wrong.'

Transgenics

At present five techniques are used to produce transgenic animals.

(1) Microinjection

The first stage involves harvesting fertilized eggs from the desired animal. At its most brutal, the animal may be slaughtered and the eggs collected. Alternatively the oviducts, which receive the eggs from the ovary, may be sliced out and the embryos removed. It is also possible to collect eggs from slaughterhouse animals and fertilize them *in vitro*. The eggs are then injected with several hundred copies of the gene just before the nucleus from the sperm has fused with that of the egg. The embryos are then transferred into the recipient animal. In cattle, the embryos are often reared for a few days in an intermediate creature, such as a sheep or a rabbit, to screen out the unviable ones. This cuts down on the numbers of 'wasted' cattle, which are expensive.

Just as it sounds, microinjection is a hit-and-miss affair.

About 10 per cent of the eggs from sheep and cattle survive and of these only 10 per cent are transgenic, and only 30–60 per cent of those exhibit any trace of the desired characteristics.

(2) The Avian Strain

For many years genetically engineering chickens was a problem but, driven by the prospect of vast profits from the birds in the broiler sheds and battery cages, the ever-resourceful agricultural researchers came up with a clever solution: the required genes are inserted into the genetic material of a virus, which then infects the birds and carries it to the nuclei of the chicken's cells. As the virus integrates its genes with the genetic material of the host – to reproduce itself – it also inserts the gene desired by the researchers. But there are many, and potentially dangerous, drawbacks to this approach. Once again, the engineers have no control over where the gene will integrate into the host DNA. Vital genes can be mutated or knocked out completely. The gene – may overproduce the desired product and damage the host – or it may not be expressed at all.

There are few reports of transgenic farm animals being produced using a virus to carry a useful gene. Avian leukosis virus has been used in chickens. Feline leukaemia virus – which causes cancer in cats – have been used in sheep and an American group has modified a chicken virus to carry genes into pig embryos.

New Diseases from Old

Ideally the virus infects the host, integrates the desired gene, then dies a quiet death and, to achieve this, the virus is crippled so that it cannot reproduce. However, viruses have been honed by millions of years of evolution to survive and reproduce as effectively as possible: they can 'revert' and begin to reproduce, which means that the hybrid virus, containing the desired gene, is free to reproduce and spread disease with unknown consequences. Even worse, it can potentially cross with others in the animal's body and create an entirely new disease. An even more disturbing but less likely possibility also exists: the genetic material of many animal species is littered with viral genes, some of which may have infected their ancestors thousands if not millions of years ago and which have achieved the ultimate feat of becoming part of their hosts. They are the perfect parasites. They also form a potential reservoir of useful information for a man-made virus. The genome of any creature is like a huge library with all the information a young, thrusting disease could wish for. All it takes is for a succession of unlikely events to occur and an old disease could be resurrected or a new one created. Viruses are always evolving in their hosts, picking up stretches of DNA, and nature is always unconsciously searching for new varieties of life. But with the creation of unstable viruses, driven by nature to reproduce, it is only a matter of time before a new or more virulent disease evolves. The possibility has already deterred some scientists from pursuing this avenue of research. For the drug companies who wish to create transgenic animals, engineered viruses represent another means of modifying a creature to enhance its value.

(3) Destroying the Function of Selected Genes

In the near future a powerful engineering tool that allows scientists to knock out a gene selectively and prevent it from functioning is likely to come to the fore. If, for example, the function of the gene which suppresses growth-hormone production could be destroyed, the benefits to the factory farmer could be immense. In theory, the animal's growth rate would increase. Essentially, the gene coding for somatostatin, which suppresses growth-hormone production, will be modified, so that it no longer works, and then injected into a recipient cell. The damaged gene will then home in on the functioning version and, during cell reproduction, should replace it in one of the resulting cells. After two cell generations some cells will contain only the damaged version of the gene. In principle, some of these embryo cells should then produce fully functioning animals with higher levels of growth hormone.

(4) Building New Chromosomes

The armoury of the genetic engineer is expanding fast but it still allows the transfer of only one or two genes per generation. Genetic engineers are still largely failing to come to grips with the complexities of transferring and controlling even one or two genes – but they are rapidly becoming more skilful. One technique offers the possibility of transferring large numbers of genes together and holds out the prospect of controlling them more precisely. In principle, it is much more efficient to transfer genes as part of a mini-chromosome, which behaves just like its larger brethren and can contain large numbers of genes. As far as the cell is concerned it is just another chromosome. Several research groups have already produced mice containing mini-chromosomes and it is likely that this technique will become the favoured route for genetically modifying animals because it will offer a greater degree of control over the end result. It is likely to be repeatable and the resulting animals may only need to be screened using a microscope – the chromosomes are large enough to be visible – to see whether they are inside the cells.

(5) Sperm Engineering

Another way of introducing a modified gene into an animal is first to introduce it into a sperm cell. When this fuses with an egg cell – to fertilize it – the gene may become part of the resulting embryo's genetic make-up. Technologies are being developed to allow breeders to transfer genes only to specific tissues or organs, which can be achieved by modifying a virus that infects only certain parts of the body. Breeders are already considering the possibilities of modifying udders to increase milk yields or to enhance its quality. Patents have already been taken out on a method of bombarding mammalian cells with tiny particles of gold or tungsten coated DNA, which is already widely used to produce transgenic plants.

The Future: the Economist and the Engineer

Within the next decade animal breeding based around genetic engineering is unlikely to displace the conventional approach. Conventional breeding has already massively increased the productivity of farm animals but the dairy cow, for example, has not yet been bred to its genetic and physiological limit, although the advent of the genetically engineered milk-boosting hormone BST may push it beyond those limits. Throughout the 1960s, the productivity of the dairy cow increased by 3–4 per cent per year. It is now increasing by 'only' 1–2 per cent a year.

There is also considerable scope for boosting the productivity of the battery laying hen. The theoretical maximum productivity of the hen is about one 2-ounce egg per day; the average bird now produces 300 eggs per year. As the hen approaches its present theoretical maximum, genetic engineering will step in to raise it. There is still considerable scope for boosting the productivity of broiler hens and pigs but, in relative terms, the sheep has hardly been touched by the breeder.

When conventional breeding begins to falter the engineer will be in the wings to increase animal production and to design creatures for new purposes and new products. At the moment genetic engineers work in the dark by trial and error but slowly, in biotech labs across the world, the animal kingdom is being remoulded to suit humanity's purposes. So far, there have been a few successes that may be valuable to humans but there have been many more disasters for the animal kingdom.

The genetic engineering of creation is driven by economics. Animals are used because it is profitable to do so. This principle holds true in the research laboratory and on the farm. The Organization for Economic Co-operation and Development (OECD), a college of the world's top economists and forecasters that advises national governments on economic and policy issues, recently produced an analysis of the impact that biotechnology will have on agriculture.[23] It says that in the foreseeable future animals will be manipulated in five main areas. The direct genetic engineering of physiology is likely to form only a small part of the way in which biotechnology affects animals but 'The uneven degree of industrialization of the main protein sources (beef, poultry, pork, fish) expresses itself in a great variety of options for incorporating biotechnology into industrial strategy.' Quaint as ever, the OECD's attitude to sentient creatures is to regard them as poorly industrialized and ripe for further exploitation as protein sources.

The Likely Areas of Manipulation

(1) Increasing the levels and types of nutrients in animal feeds.

(2) Increasing animal growth and milk production.

(3) Improving animal health.

(4) Embryo multiplication: for example, the rapid multiplication of 'superior' animals.

(5) Transgenesis: transferring desirable traits from one animal species to another.

Looking at the longer term, and also with a keen eye to economics, Professor John Webster, of Bristol University, predicts that animals will be manipulated in a further six areas:

(1) Altering an animal's digestion to increase nutrient availability.

(2) Manipulation of an animal's metabolism to increase the production of milk, meat or wool.

(3) Increasing the reproductive rate in females.

(4) Manipulation of animal consciousness.

(5) Insertion of human genes to make animals produce pharmaceuticals.

(6) Insertion of human genes into animals so that they can serve as organ donors.

Several distinct issues emerge from these predictions:

(1) Manipulating Digestion and the Food Supply

Altering an animal's digestion to increase nutrient availability conjures up images of grazing chickens and pigs. Research at Newcastle University aims to do just that.[24] How the pig would cope with it is another matter. The idea appears simple: the genes from the fibre-digesting bacteria found in the rumen of cows and sheep would be introduced into pigs and chickens. Both cows and sheep are capable of digesting cellulose – the hard fibrous material found in plants – but many animals. including humans, pigs and chickens, cannot digest it. In theory, if successful, a whole new range of fibre-digesting ruminants could be created.

However, to produce a grazing pig takes more than a sprinkling of new genes. The animal's entire make-up would need to be re-engineered: the digestion of plant fibre first requires a large vat-like stomach to ferment the mixture of celluloses and enzymes; then the animal's genetically pre-programmed instincts may need to be rewired to cope with the new food sources. The intermediate 'steps', which will, of course, be sentient creatures, produced before this research comes to fruition – if it ever does – may suffer enormously.

(2) More from the Same: Increasing Meat, Milk and Wool Production

Scientists are also trying to engineer increases in milk, meat and wool production. The animals produced by and during this research may suffer from significant welfare problems: according to the Farm Animal Welfare Council, problems may arise from the 'manipulation of body size, shape or reproductive capacity by breeding, nutrition, hormone therapy or gene insertion in such as way as to reduce mobility, increase the risk of injury, metabolic disease, skeletal or obstetric problems'. The Council's concerns read like the end product of much genetic research.

Growth-hormone genes were the first to be transferred and expressed in animals. In 1982 the first 'super-mice' were produced: these creatures were dramatically larger than normal and their creators expected to use the same techniques to grow bigger farm animals.[25] But their success has not been repeated in other species. With super-mice it was possible to control the levels of growth hormone by manipulating dietary factors such as zinc. In other species, this has not been possible. Similar experiments involving the transfer of growth-hormone genes from humans and cows to sheep produced no increase in the growth rate. The experiment also failed in another important aspect: the resulting animals' joints were painfully deformed, they suffered from a diabetes-like condition and, perhaps mercifully, they died young. In pigs, similar experiments produced animals with gastric ulcers, liver and kidney damage, bone and joint problems. Eventually, the creatures suffered from lameness, lack of co-ordination, increased incidence of pneumonia, damaged vision and a diabetes-like condition. In one infamous experiment conducted by the US Department of Agriculture, a herd of pigs was genetically engineered to grow faster but produced their human-growth hormone in the wrong tissues and ended up with crippling arthritis, deformed skulls, poor vision and, unsurprisingly given their undoubted misery, impotence and a high susceptibility to stress.[26] The Australians seem particularly keen on transgenic pigs and are currently conducting commercial trials with about 150. If the creatures prove a commercial success they will be marketed for meat.

Scientists are also working on a vaccine against the substance which inhibits the production of growth hormone. If the body's defences can be turned against the growth-hormone inhibitor then more growth-hormone should be produced and the animals should grow faster. Another trick is to turn the body's immune system against its own fat cells to produce a leaner carcass, which, according to the OECD, offers 'yet another approach to the improvement of meat quality'.

Despite the horror stories and public concern, the OECD experts are sanguine about the public's perception of animals engineered for faster growth and a greater profit margin for the farmer. The OECD will play a significant role in ensuring an international free market for these sentient 'agricultural products'. They say: 'As to the question of whether techniques to change hormone concentrations in animals are natural, it is interesting to note that king poodles contain much higher concentrations of IGF-1 [a growth promoting factor] than miniature poodles, which have higher levels than toy poodles. Dog breeders appear to have selected naturally and unknowingly for the gene coding for IGF-1 over many generations! Perhaps what is considered natural is in reality merely what has become familiar.'[27] That may be true, but it also furnishes a million excuses to degrade animal life further, with no real purpose other than profit. The only hope left to animals is that people who are capable of defending their rights do not become habituated to the emerging status quo.

Featherless Chickens

Merck and Co have patented a transgenic chicken (although they have now withdrawn the patent) with an increased growth rate and enhanced lean-to-fat ratio, which could be an important economic advantage for the farmer trying to woo the health-conscious consumer.[28] Very little information is available on the transgenic chicken but it must be a matter for concern that it suffers many of the deformities associated with the already enormous growth rate of conventional broiler chickens, which are big enough for market at 42 days. They already grow too fast for their own legs, and are in constant pain because of it, so a further raising of the growth rate without at least a corresponding increase in leg strength could condemn millions more birds to agony.

Researchers in Israel are trying to develop a featherless chicken, the rationale, again, economic. Producing feathers uses up food energy so if that energy could be redirected into growth, or not consumed at all, then the yearly savings for a farmer could be considerable. It would also allow the poultry-farming industry to mount a head-to-head challenge to the welfare lobby: if the birds could survive only on an intensive farm and not outside in the farmyard, then how could anyone insist that the birds should have access to fresh air and blue sky?

Self-shearing Sheep

The humble sheep, long neglected by breeders, is also facing the hungry gaze of the genetic engineer with Australia at the forefront of attempts to increase wool production. One of the limiting factors in wool growth, which is made up largely of the protein keratin, is the supply of two key amino acids, cysteine and methionine. Proteins are constructed from a combination of about twenty amino acids; different species of animal have their own requirements for these protein building blocks. Those that an animal cannot produce are known as 'essential amino acids' because they must be consumed in the diet. Methionine and cysteine are essential to sheep. Supplying these in the diet is not economic so agricultural scientists are trying to engineer sheep to produce their own. The production of cysteine from serine, a non-essential amino acid, required only two genes and researchers are trying to transfer these into sheep from bacteria. One team has produced transgenic mice that express the genes. Another has produced sheep that express them in their tails. Work is continuing to determine whether they can be expressed in the walls of the rumen, which is of paramount importance if the new sheep are to be economically viable.

Dr Kevin Ward, manager of the Wool Biotechnology

Programme, part of CSIRO in Australia, says that the aim of the research is to 'reduce the sheep population' by boosting the productivity of the national flock. 'We have 160 million sheep in Australia and I think that is far too many. I would dearly like to see 80 million sheep which would be possible if we can make sheep twice as efficient,' he says.[29] It may not be quite so simple. If more wool can be produced from the same number of sheep the price will drop and new uses will be developed for the fibre. Australia may well end up with a similar number of sheep, as will the rest of the world, in order to maintain the same revenue. The net result will be that shepherds will be forced to work their animals even harder. This problem may be particularly acute in sheep because a large part of their metabolism is already directed towards wool production. If wool growth is substantially increased, there is a real risk that the animal's general well-being may be reduced because essential nutrients are diverted away from bodily maintenance. Before long, sheep metabolism may become as unbalanced as that of dairy cows on drugs, both legal and illegal.

Australian researchers have also tried to develop self-shearing sheep. If the animals are injected with epidermal growth factor – a genetically engineered hormone which induces breaks in the wool fibres as they grow – then all the wool fibres will break off at their base at the same time. The idea is to produce a fleece that falls off the animal's back whereupon it can be collected by the farmer: self-shearing sheep could be far more cost-effective than conventional ones. But the ewes receiving the growth hormone suffered a one-in-five chance of spontaneous abortion and, once their woolly coats fell off, suffered from sunburn and heat stress. At present in the research station, sheep are wrapped in netting to keep the wool on their backs long enough for a new fleece to grow and protect them from the sun.[30]

Conventional shearing can be traumatic for sheep. If the side-effects of using the hormone can be eliminated – which seems unlikely – then the net result may be a positive contribution to animal welfare. Yet, if the economic costs of an increased abortion rate, sunburn and heat stress can be reduced sufficiently, the net result would be serious lowering of welfare standards.

Milk production is also likely to be boosted through biotechnology. The advantages and disadvantages of BST to increase milk production were discussed in Chapter Two. Centuries of selective breeding have already pushed the milk cow near to its productive limit but, as we saw earlier, the cow is expected to reach its genetic limit around the year 2000 so will have to be substantially re-engineered if the year-on-year increases in productivity are to continue.

Genetically engineered porcine somatotropin (PST), the pig equivalent of BST, is also likely to enter the farmer's armoury: according to the OECD, this hormone reduces body fat by up to 80 per cent and improves the efficiency of feed-use by 20 per cent.

The equivalent hormones for sheep and chickens may soon boost the profit margins of farmers and drug companies, and erode still further the welfare of the animals.

(3) Enhancing Disease Resistance

Engineering for disease resistance is one area in which the animals could benefit. There could be few objections to the work if the experiments necessary to develop it were not too gruesome. On the surface, there is a strong incentive to boost animal health: billions of pounds are lost each year worldwide through animal sickness and, not surprisingly, cattle account for most of it because they are closest to their physiological limits of production. The factory-farming industry is keen to rear healthier animals because to do so would boost profits. However, the farmer is not in a position to genetically engineer new strains of animals and the biotechnology companies are unlikely to be interested, except in isolated cases. The OECD appears tacitly to support this assumption: it envisages biotechnology's role in the short and medium term as providing only a supporting service for the farmer. In its analysis of the role of biotechnology in the agricultural and food industries, the OECD concludes that biotech firms will focus on developing diagnostic tests, vaccines and new antibiotics. The implicit assumption again is profit: there are huge margins to be made from producing a diagnostic test for a disease and supplying ways to treat it. As animals are pushed ever closer to their productive limit they will suffer ever more from productive diseases, and maintaining the profit margin depends on detecting and treating disease at the earliest possible moment. In many cases it may be more cost-effective continuously to dope the animals in the knowledge that without the treatment they will succumb to the disease. The farmer is already on this treadmill. In *Animal Welfare*, Professor Webster sums up the economic arguments against engineering healthier strains of animals thus: 'I would like to think that this was the way forward for farm animal biotechnology but I doubt it. We have here a classic example of the difference between lasting added value for society and short-term financial advantage for the entrepreneur. There is little, if any, direct profit to be made from a single action which creates a strain of animals resistant to a particular disease for all time but much potential profit to be made from developing a drug like BST designed to be injected on a regular basis into as many animals as possible.'

(4) Molecular Pharming
The arena of molecular pharming – engineering animals to produce pharmaceuticals – offers the prospect of enhancing

the welfare of both animals and humans *if the technology is exploited wisely*. In principle, virtually any molecule produced by the human body can be manufactured in an animal; if it has a therapeutic effect it can be used as a pharmaceutical. Many diseases result from either a lack or over-abundance of key molecules in the body. For example, diabetes results from a lack of the hormone insulin and many diabetics maintain their health by regularly injecting it. Insulin is now produced predominantly by bacteria but, in principle, it could be manufactured in an animal's milk and extracted ready for use. Many other diseases could also be treated by the use of human molecules manufactured in animals. Synthesizing these, even in the laboratory, is often difficult and costing and when the production process has to be scaled up to an industrial level the problems frequently increase correspondingly. Animals genetically engineered to produce these molecules offer a way round the problems.

The udders of mammals are nature's protein factories. During lactation these organs produce huge quantities of proteins and other molecules as a food for growing offspring. It is possible to hijack the animal's milk-manufacturing machinery and use it to produce high-value products. Pharmaceutical Proteins has done just that. The company was set up specifically as a molecular pharm specializing in producing the human blood-clotting factor – factor IX – and alpha 1 antitrypsin (AAT) in transgenic sheep. A deficiency of AAT can lead to emphysema. Tracey the sheep, born in 1990, was the end result of their work and produced up to 35 grams of AAT per litre of milk, worth about £2,100 after purification, which made her a very well-cared-for sheep indeed. So efficient was Tracey that AAT constituted up to 50 per cent of total protein content of the milk, which, of course, provides 'a strong impetus to the further exploitation of transgenic sheep as bioreactors for the production of large amounts of pharmacologically active proteins', said one of the researchers. Tracey and her offspring have given the company a foot in the door to a $100 million market. But, perhaps more importantly, according to Ron James, the company's managing director: 'It could not be made by any existing technology in the quantity and at the price needed to treat people.'

Pharmed Blood

Another company, DNX Corporation, of the United States, has tried to molecular pharm human haemoglobin, which is used to convey oxygen around the body, using transgenic pigs. They envisaged slaughtering 100,000 pigs a year to produce $300 million worth of haemoglobin. The DNX haemoglobin would be relatively cheap and would also be clear of human viruses such as HIV and hepatitis. But there may be other, hidden dangers. Unknown disease-causing agents, akin to that which induces BSE, could conceivably be passed to humans from the pigs, which holds true for all molecular-pharmed drugs. In 1993, due to financial constraints, DNX's work on the engineered pigs was suspended. The corporation is now focusing its efforts on producing genetically engineered pigs with hearts suitable for transplanting into humans. Time will tell whether these organs could pose a risk, real or theoretical, to human health.

Another American company, Genzyme Transgenics, is attempting to develop a compound to reduce blood-clotting in heart-attack victims. In addition, there are currently thought to be about a dozen biotech companies working on pharm animals, most of which are highly secretive operations and rarely release research results.

Tracey & Co

On balance most people would regard Tracey the engineered

sheep as a good idea. The cost to the creatures involved, so far, is minimal and they furnish great benefits to the human race. Tracey and her brethren will be treated like racehorses and receive the best of attention, simply because they are worth so much money.

But many in the animal rights movement disagree. Peter Stevenson, of Compassion in World Farming, described molecular pharming as an ethical 'grey area' and disagreed with the concept. The animals concerned are unlikely to be allowed anything like normal life, he says. They will be cocooned in sterile, stainless-steel stalls, kept clear of bedding and anything that may transmit infection – which, of course, includes their own kind. They will probably never see the sun or be allowed outside in the fresh air. The sheep engineered by Pharmaceutical Proteins are lucky: they are allowed free access to grassland – albeit double-fenced-in grassland. Most pharmed animals will not be so lucky.

But even much of molecular pharming may be unnecessary and therefore unethical. In America, trials are under way to test human-haemoglobin-like compounds produced by engineered microbes. There may be no need for engineered animals: many of the key proteins with useful properties could, in principle, be produced by plants. Odd as it may seem, from a purely biochemical viewpoint, plants have many features similar to animals: the basic way in which they manufacture proteins is essentially the same so they, too, could be used to produce new pharmaceuticals. The way that plants make proteins is far more akin to the methods used by animals than by bacteria, which is the normal port of call for the genetic engineer. Animals, however, do have one advantage for the drug companies: they have the capacity to bond sugars where biologically necessary, to the newly manufactured proteins. This feature is frequently not crucial, but even when it is, the same job could be done using conventional chemistry. Ron James puts it more simply: 'The economics for plants do not look attractive,' he says. In addition, most of the engineers involved with manufacturing new drugs prefer to work on the subjects they understand best: they are used to working on animals and are reluctant to expend the money and effort needed to refocus their attentions on engineering plants.

(5) Xenotransplantation

Imagine a pig with your heart beating inside it, your blood coursing through its veins and your immune system protecting it from infection. In twenty years this may happen. Until now, the natural response of the body's immune system to a transplanted organ from a different species has been to reduce it to blackened pulp within hours. But scientists are currently engineering pigs with human genes so that their body parts can be transplanted into people. Xenotransplantation – animal to human transplantation – is one of the hottest areas of research. A glance at the potential market shows why. DNX Corporation estimates that the market for human organs may be worth up to $6 billion per year. World demand for organs is believed to be in excess of 400,000 per year. As the Western population ages, demand for organs is likely to increase. The market is vast and growing by about 15 per cent per year while organ donations are, at best, static, and in some countries even falling. DNX Corporation is in head-to-head competition with Imutran, a British company, to lead the market in 'humanized pigs'.

But can genetic engineering deliver the goods? It's on the verge of doing so. During 1996 or early 1997 the first humanized pig hearts are expected to be transplanted into people. The engineering has been done, all the preliminary work has been completed and now the guidelines for the final state, the actual transplant programme, are being drawn up. Imutran and the surgeons at Papworth Hospital are confident of success. All the evidence indicates that the humanized pigs' hearts are capable of disarming the most virulent aspects of the body's immune system.

Theory and Practice

The human immune system is complex and the main problem in transplanting organs from pigs to humans is the violence of the immune reaction. When organs are transplanted between humans, the aggressive white cells of the immune system, known as T cells, can be handcuffed with drugs like cyclosporin. When organs are transplanted between species, however, the strength of the reaction is so powerful and immediate that within hours the immune system tears apart the foreign tissue: the cells of the foreign organs become riddled with holes punched by an immune reaction known as the complement cascade, eventually the cell contents leak away and are mopped up by other parts of the body's defences. When unleashed by the immune system this reaction, governed by a group of proteins, produces an effect 'like a bomb going off', in the words of one researcher. Drugs are useless to stop the rejection, but it can be prevented if the foreign cells are coated with pacifying proteins, which calm down the complement cascade and act rather like white flags in wartime. If the genes coding for these pacifying molecules could be transferred and expressed in other species then, in theory, organs could be transferred from animals to man. One candidate is a protein known as 'decay accelerating factor' (DAF). In human tissues this occurs on the surface of cells and wards off attacks by complement proteins.

David White, Imutran's research director and founder, has transferred the gene for DAF into pigs, which express it on their cell surfaces and appear to mute complement proteins. Pig hearts show few signs of the hyperacute rejection seen when complement proteins begin to work after human blood is pumped through the organ. The hearts have also been transplanted into cynomolgus monkeys, which act as models for humans: 20 per cent survived for more than two months and the average monkey for just over 40 days whereas unengineered pigs' hearts beat for only 55 minutes before being destroyed by the immune system. Even without the normal drug-based immune-system suppression – which is necessary to pacify the rest of the immune system – the monkeys survived on average for five days.

Rivals of the Heart

Imutran's American rival, DNX Corporation, has pursued similar methods: as well as engineering pigs to express the DAF protein, they have transferred the genes coding for two other pacifying molecules, known as CD46 and CD59. Alexion Pharmaceuticals, another American company, has designed a protein combining the properties of the two pacifying proteins DAF and CD59.

Throughout this century attempts have been made to transplant organs from one animal species to another and between 1905 and 1994 35 documented cases of animal-to-human transplants took place. All failed. One patient, 'Baby Fae', lived for 20 days after receiving a baboon's heart, but the US surgeons responsible were criticized as it appeared that no attempt had been made to find a human donor. In 1992, in California, a 26-year-old woman was given an unmodified pig's liver and died 36 hours later.

The animal experiments that laid the foundations of this work were, indeed, gruesome. In 1993, scientists at the University of Minnesota Hospital in Minneapolis transplanted pigs' hearts into baboons. The longest any of the animals survived was just 92 hours before the organ was torn apart by its immune system. Rabbits' hearts have also been transplanted into the necks of newborn piglets by scientists at Imutran. So that the results could be observed, the wounds were left open and covered with plastic film.

Before animal–man transplants become routine there are many hurdles yet to jump. The human immune system is still not fully understood and when Imutran and DNX carry out their first transplants they will be taking a huge leap in the dark. Although great financial rewards are envisaged for these companies, both insist that they will not rush their pigs to market because the last thing they need is a high-profile flop. They are aiming initially for a minimum one-year survival rate of 70–75 per cent. But they cannot predict the outcome of the first transplants. The complement cascade is an important factor but the rest of the immune system may hold yet bigger surprises for the researchers.

Yes, but Why Pigs?
Pigs were selected because their organs, especially the heart, are approximately the same size as those of an adult man. The researchers also hope that the ethical dilemmas can be reduced to that of eating streaky bacon. We eat pig's hearts so why not transplant them into a human to save a life? The ethical problems of using, say, a highly intelligent chimpanzee would be insurmountably greater. Pigs are easy and quick to breed. Primates with suitably sized organs are not.

In a report published in early 1996, the Nuffield Council on Bioethics, an organization set up to consider ethical issues raised by medicine and biology, reflects these views. On a purely biological level the ideal donors for humans would be primates, like chimpanzees and baboons, whose organs are about the right size and the immune reaction may be sufficiently mild for it to be suppressed solely with drugs. But the ethical problems would be complex and unjustifiable: the Nuffield report states that although the close relationship between humans and primates would reduce the immune reaction, it would also virtually rule out the transplants on ethical grounds: 'The close evolutionary relationship of higher primates with human beings suggests that they will share the capacity for self-awareness to the highest degree and there is good scientific evidence that this is the case.'[31]

It is the capacity in animals for self-awareness and suffering that is the cornerstone of animal-rights philosophy. The Nuffield Foundation is hardly a pro-animal-rights organization but it has sensed the prevailing public mood: the use of primate hearts would be met with such stiff opposition, not just from animal-rights groups, that it is hard to see a transplant programme ever leaving the drawing board. Also, hearts from primates can be ruled out on practical grounds, the Council says. Such is the demand for organs that suitable primates would be wiped out quickly in the wild. Their close evolutionary similarity to humans would also pose a disease threat: organs from primates could easily infect humans with new diseases. HIV, the virus which causes Aids, is believed to have originated in wild primates, as is Ebola, so this is not a purely academic worry.

Similarly, human diseases could be caught from transgenic pig organs. It is thought that the influenza that killed twenty million people in the early part of this century crossed from pigs to humans. Such devastating diseases would find it infinitely easier to cross from animals to humans if internal organs were transferred directly, especially if the patient's immune system were suppressed, as they would be during xenotransplantation. The risk of other diseases infecting humans cannot be quantified.

The Nuffield Council on Bioethics acknowledges these concerns. It said: 'Xenotransplantation of animal organs and tissue carries with it the potential risk that diseases will be transmitted from animals to xenograft recipients and to the wider human population. It is difficult to assess this risk, since it is impossible to predict whether infectious organisms that are harmless in their animal host will cause disease in human xenograft recipients or whether the disease will spread into the wider human population. There are certain to be infectious organisms of both primates and pigs that are currently unknown, and some of these might cause disease in human beings . . .

'It is not possible to predict or quantify the risk that xeno-transplantation will result in the emergence of new human diseases. But in the worst case, the consequences could be far reaching and difficult to control. The principle of precaution requires that action is taken to avoid risks *in advance* of certainty about their nature. It suggests that the burden of proof should lie with those developing the technology to demonstrate that it will not cause serious harm.'

The working party concluded that the risks had not been adequately dealt with and that human trials should not begin until they had been. It recommended that a significant amount of new research be performed before trials begin and that only organs from animals reared in near-sterile conditions be used. All patients receiving the organs should be closely monitored and an independent body should be established by the Department of Health to monitor the transplant patients.

According to the Council, before pig-heart transplants can be considered, the alternatives must be explored. The reasons are, again, ethical but when push comes to shove they are content with pig–human transplants despite their report's assertion that pigs may be sentient, self-aware beings: 'Many non-primate species, possibly including pigs, display comparable capacities of intelligence and sociality, albeit in forms that less closely resemble the human and thus appeal less strongly to human moral sensibility.'

For the animal rights movement the use of pigs as organ donors is wrong on two broad fronts: first there are legitimate ethical objections because pigs are sentient beings capable of suffering; second, there are alternatives. Mark Glover, of Respect for Animals, explains: 'There are so many alternatives to using pigs' hearts that it's just not possible to justify using them as donors. Better prevention and improved healthcare could massively reduce the demand for organs. Improving the supply of human organs through better co-ordination of the donor-card scheme and also making it an assumption that people want to donate their organs unless they specify otherwise would dramatically improve the supply. These approaches have worked in other countries so there's no reason to suppose they wouldn't work in Britain and Europe. The lack of organ transplants also results from not just a lack of suitable organs but from the sheer cost of them. Even if an inexhaustible supply suddenly appeared it's doubtful whether the medical system could cope because of the extra cost of all the ancillary healthcare that would be needed. In the longer term, technology is also likely to provide a host of alternative artificial organs that could be used to replace those from animals. In the light of all this, it's just not possible to justify the use of animals as organ donors.'

A Pig of my Own

Many engineers are already dreaming of the 'self-pig', which will be genetically tailored to individual humans – a kind of twin in pig's clothing. In the event of accident or disease, the pig's organs will be whipped out and transferred to the patient. Some are predicting that within 10–20 years the self-pig will fall within the grasp of genetic engineers. It will be a herculean task to perfect but one that is rapidly becoming feasible. The genes that govern the immune system are encoded in a huge tract of DNA known as the 'major histocompatibility complex' or MHC. To produce a self-pig would require these genes to be disabled and the equivalent area of the patient's DNA inserted. As technology advances apace, it will be possible selectively to knock out the pig MHC genes. The human genes could then be grafted into the artificial chromosomes and then injected into growing pig embryos. The most likely bottleneck with this technology is the cost: each person would need a pig or two of their own; each would need to be tended and kept disease-free. As a result, some are now pinning their hopes on pigs that could act as universal donors. But that is likely to prove extremely difficult if not impossible.

Brain cells from pig foetuses are also undergoing trials to see whether they can reverse, or at least alleviate, the symptoms of Parkinson's disease. In the early 1990s surgeons transplanted human brain cells, collected from aborted foetuses, into sufferers of Parkinson's disease but the work became embroiled in ethical arguments so medical scientists began to look at alternatives. Brain tissue is 'immunologically privileged', which means that foreign tissues are attacked less readily by the immune system. The hope is that the pig foetal tissue will not be rejected by the patients and will replace the function in Parkinson's patients of the brain cells that have been destroyed.

Other animals may also prove lucrative sources of spare parts: tissue engineering has already furnished artificial ears for children born without them. Dr Charles Vacanti, of the University of Massachusetts Medical Centre, has used mice that had been engineered to lack an immune system to grow ears on behalf of his patients. Cartilage cells from the patients were seeded onto ear-shaped plastic moulds and inserted under the skin of mice where they grew into ears ready for transplantation. Once again, there is no overriding reason to subject animals to this kind of suffering: the techniques that produced the ears grown on the backs of mice could be adapted so that patients could grow their own spare parts. It may look unsightly to have a spare ear growing on the inside of your arm but the risk of disease transmission would be eliminated and the cost reduced.

(6) Reducing Sentience

A large dairy animal approached Zaphod Beeblebrox's table, a large fat meaty quadruped of the bovine type with large watery eyes, small horns and what might almost have been an ingratiating smile on its lips.

'Good evening,' it lowered and sat back on its haunches, 'I am the main Dish of the Day. May I interest you in parts of my body?' It harrumphed and gurgled a bit, wriggled its hindquarters into a more comfortable position and gazed peacefully at them.

Its gaze was met by startled looks of bewilderment from Arthur and Trillian, a resigned shrug from Ford Prefect and naked hunger from Zaphod Beeblebrox. 'Something off the shoulder perhaps?' suggested the animal. 'Braised in a white wine sauce?'

'Er, *your* shoulder?' asked Arthur in a horrified whisper.

'But naturally my shoulder, sir,' mooed the animal contentedly, 'nobody else's is mine to offer.'

Zaphod leapt to his feet and started prodding and feeling the animal's shoulder appreciatively.

'Or the rump is very good,' murmured the animal. 'I've been exercising it and eating plenty of grain, so there's a lot of good meat there.' It gave a mellow grunt, gurgled again and started to chew the cud. It swallowed the cud again. 'Or a casserole of me perhaps?' it added.

'You mean this animal actually wants us to eat it?' whispered Trillian to Ford.

'Me?' said Ford, with a glazed look in his eyes. 'I don't mean anything.'

'That's absolutely horrible,' exclaimed Arthur, 'The most revolting thing I've ever heard.'

'What's the problem, Earthman?' said Zaphod, now transferring his attention to the animal's enormous rump.

'I just don't want to eat an animal that's standing there

inviting me to,' said Arthur, 'it's heartless.'

'Better than eating an animal that doesn't want to be eaten,' said Zaphod.

'That's not the point,' Arthur protested. Then he thought about it for a moment. 'All right,' he said, 'maybe it is the point. I don't care, I'm not going to think about it now. I'll just . . . er . . .' . . . 'I think I'll just have a green salad,' he muttered.

'May I urge you to consider my liver?' asked the animal, 'it must be very rich and tender by now, I've been force-feeding myself for months.'

'A green salad,' said Arthur emphatically.

'A green salad?' said the animal, rolling his eyes disapprovingly at Arthur.

'Are you going to tell me,' said Arthur, 'that I shouldn't have green salad?'

'Well,' said the animal, 'I know many vegetables that are very clear on that point. Which is why it was eventually decided to cut through the whole tangled problem and breed an animal that actually wanted to be eaten and was capable of saying so clearly and distinctly. And here I am . . . I'll just nip off and shoot myself.'

He turned and gave a friendly wink to Arthur.

'Don't worry, sir,' he said, 'I'll be very humane . . .'

The Restaurant at the End of the Universe, Douglas Adams

Animals may soon be engineered into mindless lumps of meat. When it happens, will it be OK to eat them? Is it right to eat 'dumb' farm animals but not highly intelligent chimpanzees, or is there no ethical difference? This dilemma may soon loose itself upon the consumer. Scientists studying the genetic basis of intelligence have discovered that damaging, or deleting, certain genes in rats makes them less able to learn from experience. These 'thick' rats can make on-the-spot decisions to avoid pain, for instance, but seem unable to learn from the experience even if it involves avoiding immense discomfort. Their memory appears significantly impaired and, according to most definitions, their sentience is reduced.

The basis of animal rights – and also most concepts of welfare – is sentience. We have no right to inflict pain or suffering on sentient creatures because they have the intelligence to be aware of pain and of their own existence. They have innate value. If sentience is reduced, do we have the right to inflict pain and suffering on the newly created animal? If the intellect of a cow is reduced to that of a grasshopper then, in theory, taking its life would be less unethical than killing the more intelligent unmodified cow. Ethical discussions are intellectual minefields at the best of times and the implications of reducing sentience are even more so. Logically it would appear kinder to produce animals of extremely low intelligence for our food. That way they would not suffer and humanity would get its much cherished flesh. However, the perversity of reducing an intelligent, gentle creature to little more than a plant seems deeply immoral to many philosophers.

The Reverend Professor Andrew Linzey, holder of the world's first academic post in the theological and ethical aspects of animal welfare at Oxford University, abhors the idea. The basis for his theological defence of animal rights is the recognition that animals have intrinsic value of God's creatures. Even if their self-awareness is destroyed by man, they still have rights on the basis of their God-given worth. Eliminating sentience is, therefore, morally wrong. He says: 'It was Aristotle's dream to do this. He hoped that one day slaves would do as they were bid and we could organize nature so that nature did as we bid it. It's an ancient dream and now, unfortunately, with biotechnology, it's becoming a reality.

'Failure to accept that we have certain limits in relation to animals, in terms of suffering and pain, has led us to disrespect their nature. Many biotechnologists really have no notion of there being an animal nature at all, let alone there being one that they should respect. Animals have the right to be animals. Once one claims the right to redesign them then one is doing something that challenges their integrity. The genetic engineers are suggesting that there is nothing in nature that has integrity. I think that is very problematic. I do think that it threatens human nature and the human species as well. If it's true that there is no nature that needs to be respected, of any kind, however you interpret that, then why stop at animals? The same people who are genetically engineering farm animals really don't see a problem in principle with genetically engineering human beings. Public consciousness has not recognized the far-ranging science of genetic engineering. For instance, why stop at engineering out disabilities from the human population? Alcoholism, wife-beating, homosexuality, political dissidents – all could be dealt with. If scientists and politicians are given that kind of power – absolute power – then the whole technology becomes even more disturbing.'

Such sentiments are often treated disparagingly by biotechnologists. They are dismissed simply as another 'yuk factor' with no sound scientific basis. Animals are there to be used and so long as they are not treated with 'unnecessary cruelty' then it is permissible to carry on using them. This argument failed to impress the MAFF committee set up to investigate the ethical implications of the emerging animal-breeding technologies. The committee warned that ' . . . the fact that the objection is often stated in emotional terms is not sufficient reason for discounting it: revulsion or disgust at certain uses of animals may be perfectly rational and founded upon a conviction . . . as to the intrinsic wrongness of what is proposed.' It went on to warn that the use of animals which failed 'to respect the natural characteristics, dignity and worth of animals' would be deeply objectionable.[32] Clearly, reducing the intelligence of farm animals falls into this category of abuse.

But there are also practical animal-welfare arguments against reducing sentience. Because we know precious little about the nature of sentience, we cannot judge the level of an animal's awareness. Witness the recent disturbing findings that humans in a persistent vegetative state – which by most definitions are dead – are often dimly aware of themselves and their surroundings, and some have even tried to communicate with loved ones. Animals with reduced sentience may end up in a similar state except they may well be trapped even more keenly in a living hell. The experiments performed so far on rats have concentrated only on the most obvious aspects of self-awareness: if a creature is unable to remember the past then logically it should have only a limited awareness of its own existence. If an animal exists solely in the here and now, then surely it cannot have the wherewithal to realize that in the immediate future it may be slaughtered? This rather cosy scenario would allow the meat industry to reduce the sentience of its products so that ethical arguments against the industry could be brushed aside: animals could be reduced to just chunks of pulsating flesh, with a nutrient feed, waste outlet, and electrical stimulation periodically to tense the muscles to produce the necessary juicy meat.

In a metaphorical sense, this strategy has paid off handsomely over the last fifty years for the Meat and Livestock Commission and its predecessors. They have sought to convince the consumer that meat does not involve suffering because it is only meat – not an animal that was once living. It is a strategy that they cherish.

When the Countryside Movement was launched in the autumn of 1995, it pledged to re-establish in the urban mind the reality of country living. With the help of a £3.5 million advertising campaign they aimed to educate the urban consumer in the realities of rural life. Top of their list was a defence of hunting and also of the meat industry. They feared that urban dwellers were unaware of the – quite ridiculous – 'need' for fox-hunting and also of the realities of meat production. Part of their campaign aimed to re-establish the link between slabs of flesh and farm animals and one of the adverts featured a smiling man, dressed in a pearly white smock, meat cleaver in pocket, with the slogan: 'George Roberts, head slaughterman and animal lover'. The animal rights movement was delighted, the Meat and Livestock Commission livid. It has spent decades in slowly breaking the link between rearing and slaughtering animals and the flesh at the end of the process.

But people are now beginning to care about animals as living entities and not as food. Mark Glover, of the hard-hitting animal rights group Respect for Animals, described the Countryside Movement's campaign as a gift to the Animal Rights Movement.

Reducing an animal's apparent intellect may not reduce its real sentience or its capacity to suffer. It may be possible even to eliminate sentience but it is not possible to make animals themselves worthless as creations. Jeremy Bentham, the eighteenth-century philosopher, based his defence of animals on the basis of their capacity to experience pain.

If an animal's intellect is reduced it will not cease to exist so it will feel pain as acutely as any of its unmodified brethren. But the pain may be even worse. Second by second it will perpetually rediscover the pain and horror of the factory farm: instead of becoming numbed to the tedium and the discomfort, these creations may constantly rediscover it. Reducing sentience may have an even darker side: instead of improving the conditions of farm creatures it may allow the industry to destroy their concept of quality. These creatures will be moulded to the environment and not the environment to them. They will be reduced further to a state of worthlessness.

10

Patenting Life

Drug companies and their agricultural research arms are spending tens of millions of pounds on developing the new animals – or 'products' as they prefer to call them. These are their future revenue streams. If a company spends £50–100 million in developing a new drug produced in an animal, they want to be certain of freezing out the opposition who may make the engineered products at knock-down prices. In short, they want a monopoly to exploit their creations. The drug companies have managed to stretch patent laws to incorporate living sentient creatures that have been engineering by man.

The protection of intellectual property is the oil between the wheels of the capitalist machine. Electronic or printed information – this book, for instance – is copyright protected: it cannot be copied without the permission of the copyright holder who will normally charge a fee for its reproduction. Inventions – for example, a new type of toaster or a drug for treating arthritis – are covered by patents, which furnish protection against unauthorized copying. Over the last five years there has been a rush to treat genetically engineered animals as inventions and to patent them. Since 1991 there has been an unseemly rush to patent human genes for private profit as well.

According to Nick Scott-Ram, chairman of the BioIndustry Association's intellectual property committee, patents are vital if pharmaceutical and agricultural companies are to continue their research and bring new products to market. 'The time scale for developing a new drug may be 10 years and it may cost £100 million. If anybody can then come along and copy it then the chances are the company won't develop the product in the first place,' he says. The OECD agrees: it says that patents have 'become essential to the industrial development and diffusion of agricultural biotechnology. Patent protection is one of the main conditions for a sufficient financial return on R&D [research and development] investments, and hence its adequacy does play a role in company decisions on agricultural biotechnology.'[33] Apparently, the United States affords 'better conditions' for biotechnology because it allows animals to be patented almost as a matter of routine. Europe, however, is more troublesome because it allows objections to such patents on moral grounds.

The storm over patenting animals erupted in 1992 when the European Patent Office (EPO) announced it was granting a provisional patent for the 'oncomouse'. This creature looks and behaves like any other mouse but has a cancer gene stitched into its DNA. This 'oncogene' – from *onco*logy – dooms the animal to die from cancer. It is the first animal to be designed to suffer and die from cancer no matter how well it is treated. It has 'utility', in the language of the patent lawyers, in cancer research. The patent, if finally granted, would allow an array of other onco-animals such as oncorabbits, oncodogs and oncomonkeys, to be created and sold. Harvard University, which is seeking to patent the animal, wants to profit from this research and sell the mouse as if it was any other piece of laboratory equipment. When the EPO announced its decision to grant the patent, more than 200 organizations including German Christian churches, environmentalists and animal-welfare groups banded together to lodge 17 objections.

According to Peter Stevenson, political and legal director of Compassion in World Farming, the battle over the onco-mouse 'is a critical test case'. 'If the oncomouse patent goes through, you'll see lots of applications for patents on farm animals for increased productivity.' The benefits to cancer research are at best marginal, Stevenson argues, and the EPO did not consider the animal-welfare issues and the ramifications of allowing, in effect, a whole new range of onco-animals to be created.

The welfare groups object to the patent on moral grounds because it would mean profiting directly from an animal's suffering. But they are most fearful of the wider implications involved in patenting animals: they are acutely aware that if they don't win this one then all classes of farm animals are likely to be engineered in the future – not just for enhanced productivity but for a whole plethora of different, as yet unknown, uses. Farm-animal welfare may become even more compromised. Stevenson says, 'Through traditional selective breeding alone, chickens grow twice as fast as they did thirty years ago. Many of today's farm animals are pushed to their physiological limits. Why push it even further with genetic engineering? We don't need transgenic superchickens.'

Religious groups oppose patenting because it institutionalizes animal suffering and because it infringes what they see as the integrity of creation. The Reverend Professor Andrew Linzey says, 'Animals are God's creatures. We do not own them, they are not human artefacts or inventions and they must not be treated simply as means to human ends. To class them as inventions is a category mistake. We have been given dominion over the world but dominion is not despotism. Humans are meant to be God's deputies in creation, reflecting God's care for creation. We really must get away from the medieval idea that the whole earth is made simply for human use. If patenting animals is allowed it will mark the lowest status granted to animals in the history of European ethics. The truth is that some people have given up believing in God and have begun to deify themselves. We have to rediscover certain fundamental moral limits to what we can do to animals and this can only be achieved by changing our view of ourselves in creation.'

It all comes down to semantics and defensible positions. Patenting animals is emotive. Patenting what you have done to them is less so. Hence, Dr Nick Scott-Ram asks: 'What is life anyway? I don't regard DNA as life. It's really a chemical that can be synthesized. How do you define life? Every chemical in the body has the essence of it. Some people say it's the DNA but I don't agree. It has the information for life. Not life itself.'

Patents are immensely important for the emerging biotechnology industry. Each year it spends more than $100 million in protecting intellectual property. But engineered animals posed a problem for the industry: they have been excluded from the patenting system for hundreds of years, long before, of course, even the concepts of genetic engineering were dreamt of. Life was considered a product of nature and inherently unpatentable.

But then the scent of vast profits wafted under the noses of biotech-industry executives. In 1980 the US Supreme Court ruled that 'anything under the sun that is made by man' could be patented. The ruling followed an intense battle by Ananada Chakrabarty to patent a type of bacteria engineered to break down some of the components of crude oil. He believed it could be a lucrative way of profiting from oil spills. The US Patent Office initially refused to grant one but the Supreme Court reversed the decision because the bacteria were not naturally occurring. But what principally angers many who oppose animal patents is the Supreme Court refusal to hear any moral objections to the bacteria patent. The judgement was made strictly to the letter of the law. In 1987 the US Patent Office widened the criteria still further and said it would accept applications for higher forms of life than bacteria. The floodgates had been opened not only to patenting animals but also human genes.

But Europe is different. Under the European Patent Convention, Clause 53a, patents can be refused on the grounds of public order or morality. This is a chink in the armour of the biotech industry and both sides know it. Patent protection is the most vital step in bringing a product to market: without it, rival companies can quickly produce the same thing cheaper. That is why the biotech industry and animal-rights groups are taking this battle so seriously. 'Everybody is focusing on patents because they are easy to shoot down,' says Nick Scott-Ram.

In 1992 the OECD warned industrialists that 'a new tendency should be noted'. 'Official patent circles and the industries that utilize biotechnology do not question the appropriateness of intellectual property for the new processes and products that emerge from the research and that show commercial promise. A highly vocal challenge to this assumption has come from animal rights and green movements and their supporters in the political arena and elsewhere. Taking a stand on the alleged unethical practice of 'patenting life', these groups often extend their opposition to any significant structural change in the agricultural industry that might arise from biotechnology and especially from the acquisition in the hands of multinational companies of monopoly rights on the advances that are being made. This argument is applied to both plant and animal biotechnology and in the latter case a moral objection is also raised against interference with the assumed right to integrity of the species. This opposition is targeted against the patenting of these inventions no less than against the research itself. The opposers have clearly appreciated the role of patent protection in stimulating the funding of this research, and their strategy is clear. This movement is highly active in the United States and in the European Parliamentary system and can be expected to maintain a high profile in the public debate for some time to come.'[34]

Then, as now, multinational corporations wishing to assert their 'monopoly rights' over the newly engineered animals are unsure of the power and influence of the environmental and animal rights movements.

The OECD asked: 'Could opposition of the public or of minority groups, working through parliamentary and other procedures, spill over into the legislative and legal process and prevent the required modifications [the extending] of patent law regarding biotechnology?' It concluded that the multinationals would eventually achieve their desired result – patenting the newly created animals and achieving 'monopoly rights' over them – but hinted that 'opposition could cause further delay, particularly in Europe'. The 'minority groups' and those active in the 'Parliamentary system' – the elected representatives of the people of Europe – are still causing delay and intend to carry on doing so.

PART THREE

What Does It All Mean?

11

Animals are Worthless:
the Traditional View

Animals are eaten, worn, poisoned, impaled, blown up, crushed, drowned, torn up, mutilated, tortured and driven insane, all in the name of science and economics, because they do not have the power to defend themselves. They have no value and cannot fight to liberate themselves as humans have done. They are treated as mere commodities without feelings or rights. How can we let this happen?

Animal abuse occurs because society allows it and it will continue to do so unless four barriers can be surmounted: ignorance; the vested interests of the meat industry; science; and philosophy, including religion. The public's ignorance has long been bliss for the meat trade but it is rapidly being dispelled. Live animal transport has been brought to the edge of extinction because the public took action when they saw livestock trucks rolling through small towns like Shoreham and Brightlingsea. People saw the horror and acted. The same could happen to the meat industry, which is painfully aware that the ground is being cut from underneath it and intends to fight to keep the profits rolling in. The Meat and Livestock Commission currently spends about £10 million per year persuading people to continue to buy meat while others with vested interests in selling meat and dairy products spend tens of millions more. But health concerns and the growing realization that cruelty is endemic in the industry is encouraging the public to move away from meat like never before. During the decade to 1995 the number of vegetarians more than doubled to about 6 per cent of the UK population and is still growing rapidly. Between 10 and 20 per cent of young people now eat no meat and more are giving it up in ever greater numbers. Animal rights is the issue of the twenty-first century and the meat industry will not long be able to withstand the pressure for change.

Animal-rights philosophy is now seen as a legitimate area of thought: it is grounded, first, on the logic underlying Darwin's theory of evolution, which taught that human and non-human animals are fundamentally similar; and, second, on the premise that there are no moral grounds for using or mistreating animals. Animal-rights philosophy is based on the understanding that animals think, feel and suffer, that, consequently, they have the right not to be tortured and killed for trivial reasons. In short, they, like humans, are sentient creatures with rights.

Thirty years ago these ideas were revolutionary but are now becoming increasingly mainstream and the focus has shifted from arguments about the legitimacy of the philosophy to its effects on human thought and society. Science, however, is still in a logical bind on animal rights: the views of the researcher are still guided more by two millennia of religion and philosophy, which taught that animals have no moral or ethical significance, than by straightforward logic. A central tenet of science is that the thoughts and beliefs of a researcher should be excluded from an experiment, which prevents their preconceptions from becoming entangled with and distorting the results. It is sound science. However, researchers working with animals are intensely aware that should the charge of anthropomorphism – the projection onto animals of human thoughts, feelings and emotions – be laid against their work, the results will be seen as worthless.

Objective science relies on excluding the views of the researcher to establish hard, repeatable facts. But this approach fails when an attempt is made to study the mental similarities between human and non-human animals. The qualities that are the essence of sentience such as rational thought, feeling and emotion, are excluded from the study of animal minds. In the eyes of the scientific establishment, to take them into account would bias an experiment. It is hardly surprising that animals are denied their basic rights when any research that may shed light on the animal mind is stymied by such an array of preconceptions. The system has evolved to fit the needs of the 'hard sciences', like physics, chemistry and certain aspects of biology, where repeatable experiments can be designed. It works. But when applied to the study of the animal mind, it fails.

Stephen Clark, Professor of Philosophy at the University of Liverpool and one of the most incisive thinkers on animal rights, says that this strict approach to anthropomorphism holds dangers for the study of animal awareness: 'Objecting to anthropomorphism, or more generally objecting to a certain kind of moralistic teleological analysis, is a very good discipline. It is sometimes absolutely essential. [But] if you regard it as the only available method then you will have problems. It is sometimes unsuited to the study of animal intelligence because, right from the start, you're preventing yourself from seeing what might be there. If you start out with the view that the rest of the world is not like us then you can't show that it is like us. In other areas scientists don't start from that assumption: they start from the view that the world is a continuum – that there aren't massive barriers between different sorts of things, species for instance.'

157

Contrary to Darwin's theory of evolution, it is still accepted by many that animals are fundamentally different from humans, devoid of rational thought and incapable of emotion. But this approach is itself a bias. It says, in effect, 'Don't look for these features because they can't exist in animals', which ensures that the right questions are not asked. Science advances by asking the right questions: if you can't ask the right questions then you won't get the right answers. Only a brave few, usually working with primates, dare to try to ask the right questions.

Jane Goodall, the world leader in the study of wild chimpanzee behaviour, recalls her earlier problems: 'When, in the early 1960s, I brazenly used such words as "childhood", "adolescence", "motivation", "excitement" and "mood" [to describe the animals] I was much criticized. Even worse was my crime of suggesting that chimpanzees had "personalities": I was ascribing human characteristics to non-human animals and was thus guilty of that worst of ethological sins – anthropomorphism.'[35]

Charles Darwin had no qualms about breaking the conventions. For him, emotions and sentience could be ascribed to non-human animals. The title of one of his books says it all: *The Expression of the Emotions in Man and Animals*. Earlier, he had imagined a dog's conscious life: 'But can we feel sure that an old dog with an excellent memory and some power of imagination, as shewn by his dreams, never reflects on his past pleasures in the chase? And this would be a form of self-consciousness.' He also asked: 'Who can say what cows feel, when they surround and stare intently on a dying or dead companion?'

The scientific establishment's view of the animal mind as wholly distinct from that of the human did not spring out of thin air and malice. It grew from millennia of religious and philosophical thought, which taught that man was special and separate from the rest of creation. The accepted views of modern society developed from the same source – and the meat industry uses them to trick the consumer into thinking that there is nothing wrong in rearing, transporting and slaughtering animals in appalling conditions. When these views are held up to scrutiny they are exposed as a mere excuse for humans to pillage the planet for whatever trivial use is deemed necessary. Although scientists are beginning to challenge these deep-rooted ideas the farming industry is resistant to change. Ultimately, therefore, it is up to ordinary people to fight for animal liberation. First, however, understand the enemy.

Peter Singer, Professor of Philosophy at Monash University in Melbourne, Australia, and author of *Animal Liberation*, argues that 'the attitudes towards animals of previous generations are no longer convincing because they draw on presuppositions – religious, moral, metaphysical – that are now obsolete'. Aristotle taught that animals were made for human use, and Greek philosophy became enmeshed with that espoused in the Old Testament: God created man in his own image and told him to be 'fruitful, and multiply, and replenish the earth, and subdue it; and have dominion over the fish of the sea, and over the fowl of the air, and over every living thing that moveth upon the Earth'. But the Old Testament also encourages people to respect animals: 'The righteous man regardeth the life of his beast' says Proverbs 12:10. On balance, the Old Testament attempts to instil a respect for animals. Indeed, Genesis carries a very strong hint that humankind was vegetarian before being cast out of the Garden of Eden. God said to Eve and Adam in Genesis 1:29: 'Behold, I have given you every herb bearing seed, which *is* upon the face of all the Earth, and every tree, in which *is* the fruit of a tree yielding seed; to you it shall be for meat.'

Christianity gave somewhat less succour to the animal

kingdom. The Christian Church reached its first peak under the Roman Empire and effectively fused Greek and Roman thoughts about animals. Many of the most powerful ideas were formulated by the Greek Stoic philosophers who, from about 300 BC, organized systems of ethics that eventually asserted that animals have no value, because they cannot make contracts that bind them into a system of rights and duties. In essence, animals do not have rights because they do not have duties. The Stoics argued that rights and duties are so intertwined that the two cannot be divorced. Without rights animals were inherently worthless. In many other respects, the Stoics were strikingly modern: they were obsessed with physics, logic and ethics and how to attain objective truth. Many of their systems of logic were not surpassed until the nineteenth century and the logical systems behind numerous complex computer programmes are still based on their premises. But the darker side of their legacy is the assertion that animals are inherently worthless, which still colours modern ethical thought largely because of its effect on Christian ethics as currently practised.

Eating Flesh is Fun

In the early Christian Church, the ethics surrounding animals became even more twisted and complex. Stephen Clark says, 'The whole problem over animals became part of the sectarian divide between Pagan Platonists and Christians.

'Pagan Platonists were quite often vegetarians and concerned for animals, as were Manicheans. Manicheans were of the opinion that the world was a thoroughly rotten place made by a rather bad God. Christians were so concerned to distance themselves from this that they had to keep saying that the world is absolutely splendid and eating creatures is fun. But they went further, and said that if you don't eat creatures it must be because you're disrespectful of God. So they drew away from a fairly strong vegetarian ascetic tendency in the early years and started saying that 'you've got to prove you're a proper Christian by munching on animals'. They drew away from the fairly clear injunctions of the Old Testament [to have respect for animals] and instead emphasized their concern for human beings.'

Animals suffered particularly under the Romans, as did many Christians. Of course the basic Roman attitude to animals, a crystallization of Stoic, Roman and Christian thought, was epitomized in the 'games', during which the blood of people and animals was spilt liberally. This hardened the attitude of the populace against sympathy for the weak. In *Animal Liberation* Professor Peter Singer quotes W. E. H. Lecky, a nineteenth-century historian, on the rise of the Roman games from a combat between two gladiators to a form of ritualized carnage on a massive scale.

> The simple combat became at last insipid, and every variety of atrocity was devised to stimulate the flagging interest. At one time a bear and a bull, chained together, rolled in fierce combat across the sand; at another, criminals dressed in the skins of wild beasts were thrown to bulls, which were maddened by red-hot irons, or by darts tipped with burning pitch. Four hundred bears were killed on a single day under Caligula . . . Under Nero, four hundred tigers fought with bulls and elephants. In a single day, at the dedication of the Colosseum by Titus, five thousand animals perished. Under Trajan, the games continued for one hundred and twenty-three successive days. Lions, tigers, elephants, rhinoceroses, hippopotami, giraffes, bulls, stags, even crocodiles and serpents were employed to give novelty to the spectacle.

During the seventeenth century, René Descartes, known as the father of modern philosophy, probably did more to devalue animal life than anyone before or since: he taught that animals were sufficiently different from man for them not even to feel pain. Descartes claimed that mind and body were wholly different entities: the mind was immaterial in nature while the body was simply a complex machine. Because humans have a mind as well as a body, they could think and feel. Animals, however, were devoid of mind and therefore incapable of feeling pain. Descartes wrote, 'My opinion is not so much cruel to animals as indulgent to men . . . since it absolves them from the suspicion of crime when they eat or kill animals,' a convenient philosophical standpoint for those participating in the newly evolving study of physiology in which animals were cut up alive by the thousand so that their organs and blood circulation could be studied. So extreme were Descartes' views that a creature's screams of agony were treated as a reflex action with no more substance than the ticking of a clock. As the screams sometimes disturbed the vivisectors, the animal's vocal cords were cut, and to prevent their escape, dogs' paws were nailed to boards.

In 1738 Nicholas Fontaine wrote:

> They administered beatings to dogs with perfect indifference, and made fun of those who pitied the creatures as if they felt pain. They said the animals were clocks; that the cries they emitted when struck were only the noise of a little spring that had been touched, but that the whole body was without feeling. They nailed poor animals up on boards by their four paws to vivisect them and see the circulation of the blood which was a subject of great conversation.

But change was coming, heralded by Jeremy Bentham, who wrote, in his *Introduction to the Principles of Morals and Legislation*:

The day *may* come when the rest of the animal creation may acquire those rights which never could have been withholden from them but by the hand of tyranny. The French have already discovered that the blackness of the skin is no reason why a human being should be abandoned without redress to the caprice of a tormentor. It may one day come to be recognised that the number of the legs, the villosity of the skin, or the termination of the *os sacrum* are reasons equally insufficient for abandoning a sensitive being to the same fate. What else is it that should trace the insuperable line? Is it the faculty of reason, or perhaps the faculty of discourse? But a full-grown horse or dog is beyond comparison a more rational, as well as a more conversable animal, than an infant of a day or a week or even a month old. But suppose they were otherwise, what would it avail? The question is not, Can they *reason*? nor Can they *talk*? but Can they *suffer*?

Darwin's Revolution

Bentham may have laid the explosives under Descartes' views but it was Charles Darwin who detonated them. In *The Origin of Species*, Darwin argued that mankind was not fundamentally different from the rest of creation because life evolves through a process of natural selection. In each generation only the fittest survive and their characteristics are passed on to succeeding generations. It is how life adapts to a constantly changing environment. New species evolve from old and fit into the changing environment. As a result, all life is related. Humans are related to non-human animals: we are closely related to chimpanzees and less so, say, to marmosets and pigs. There is no physical characteristic that is unique to man. The differences and similarities between man and beasts are of degree not of kind. All animals are related to us and that includes the creatures we hunt for fun, eat for pleasure and poison for profit. Many are self-aware, capable of rational thought but, more importantly, can suffer.

When *The Origin of Species* was published in 1859 it was more than a bomb exploding in the heart of western culture: it was a vat of acid that began to eat into its core, into man's species-centred ideas of being an act of divine creation with a unique role in the universe.

With characteristic devotion Darwin advanced his thesis that mankind was not divorced from the rest of the animal kingdom virtually year on year. *The Descent of Man* further emphasized the lack of fundamental differences between human and non-human animals, as did *The Expression of the Emotions in Man and Animals*. He argued that animals experience a range of emotions including: anxiety, fear, horror, grief, despair, love, devotion, hatred, anger, contempt, disgust, guilt, pride, patience, surprise, shame, shyness and modesty. Even now, many still regard emotion, especially love, as the most likely characteristic to be uniquely human, preferring to concede that animals have a degree of intellect rather than that they could feel as we do. Surely love can be felt only by a human? Not so, according to Darwin. For him, though, the ability to reason was the critical faculty but even this, he argued, is not unique to man. However, although Darwin destroyed the intellectual foundations that allowed humans to exploit animals, he continued to eat them, and refused to sign a petition that urged the RSPCA to use its growing influence to press for legislation against animal experiments because he feared it would interfere with the advance of science.

Darwin, unwittingly or not, laid the foundation stone for the modern animal-rights movement. To those fully versed in his theory and a smattering of philosophy, the only reasons to continue using animals for food, clothing, experiments and for pleasure are selfish ones. To discriminate against animals because they are not humans is exactly the same logic that allows one tribe, sex or nation to discriminate against another. Richard Ryder, one of the founders of the modern animal-rights movement, coined the term 'speciesism', to describe it. Yet even today, a century after Darwin's death, most people still maintain: 'But animals *are* different!'

12

Modern Animal-rights Philosophy

Modern animal-rights philosophy is based on the belief that animals are sufficiently like humans for their interests to be taken into account. Humans are not separate from the rest of creation but are an integral part of it. The qualities possessed by humans are also, to a greater or lesser degree, to be found in many other animals. Consequently, if humans are accorded rights based on the principle that all races and both sexes have inherent value then the same must apply to animals. Human life is worthy of protection because it matters to that person whether they live or die and, to a lesser degree, to those close to that person. Humans have a memory of the past; they are capable of planning for the future; they are capable of rational thought; they feel pain and experience emotion. They know what life is and want to continue living; in essence, all people are born equal because they have the capacity to live a life. Many animals possess these features, and for the sake of logical consistency, if nothing else, their interests must be considered. Even if some species of animal do not possess many of the features we have come to associate with humanity, such as a high degree of rationality, they should not be denied basic rights.

According to Professor Andrew Linzey, if there are no *morally significant* differences between an animal and a human then an animal has rights that should be respected. A morally significant difference can be defined as one that has a marked bearing on the way in which a creature should be treated: the capacity to suffer or not is a morally significant difference; the size, shape, colour or even the intellect of an animal is morally *in*significant. In humans, age is a morally insignificant difference: it is no more acceptable to mistreat an elderly person than it is to beat a child. To return to Jeremy Bentham: 'The question is not, Can they *reason*? nor Can they *talk*? but Can they *suffer*?'

Animal-rights philosophy does not necessarily accord the *same* rights to animals as to humans but it demands that where human and animal interests are in conflict, weight must be given to the interests of the animal. Animal-rights philosophy demands the *equal consideration* of interests.

Professor Peter Singer says: 'If it would be absurd to give animals the right to vote, it would be no less absurd to give that right to infants or to severely retarded human beings yet we still give equal consideration to their interests: we don't test cosmetics in their eyes – nor should we. But we do these things to non-human animals who show greater abilities in using tools or communicating with each other, or doing any of the other things which use those capacities of reason that we like to believe distinguish humans from animals. Once we understand this, we may take a different view of the belief that all humans are somehow infinitely more valuable than any animal. We may see this belief for what it is: a prejudice. Such prejudices are not unusual. Racists have a similar prejudice in favour of their own race, and sexists have the same type of prejudice in favour of their own sex. Hence the term "speciesism" has been coined to refer to the prejudice many humans have in favour of their own species.'[36]

Traditionalists, however, challenge animal-rights philosophy: they claim that animals lack consciousness, the ability to think rationally, to communicate, to consent to a contract conferring both rights and duties; they believe that humans are different because they alone are 'moral' animals. Let us examine the arguments.

Animal Sentience

Descartes denied animals rights by asserting that they were not conscious and were therefore incapable of feeling pain. To suffer, he wrote, you must be aware of pain and although animals gave the impression of suffering – crying out if they were dissected alive, for instance – it was simply a reflex reaction because they have no self-awareness.

Descartes' views are now entirely discredited but we still have no clear idea about the nature of consciousness and how it originates in the individual. However, it is thought to come, broadly, in two forms: the first is the awareness of self and of one's existence, the second is the type of consciousness experienced during meditation where one is aware of the universe but not of self. But perhaps the best definition is given by the philosopher Ted Honderich, Professor of Philosophy at University College, London: 'Consciousness is elusive and trying to think about it can make you unhappy.'[37]

The origin of consciousness is equally contentious but has a bearing on the nature of animal rights. Each of the three main theories (there are, of course, many more) includes the concept of animal awareness and therefore of animal rights.

I Think But Then Again . . .

The current most fashionable theory of consciousness is also the most perplexing: it claims that consciousness is an illusion created by certain other properties of the mind, that it results from a series of complex interactions between different parts of the brain and groups of cells within it. Take this theory to its logical conclusion, and you'll discover that we are not *really* aware, we just think we are . . . Yet it provides a clear explanation of how consciousness may arise in animals. Since animal and human brains function in the same way there is no reason to deny that animals are conscious. Man and beast react in the same way to stimuli – for instance, drawing away from a source of pain and crying out. The only realistic way to deny the existence of consciousness in animals would be on the basis of brain size and complexity. Virtually all species possess a smaller brain than humans and for consciousness to arise a brain of sufficient complexity is required. But scientists have not yet established how complex 'sufficient complexity' is. If Darwin is any guide, though, it is unlikely that humanity is the only species whose brain is sufficiently complex to produce consciousness. Several species of whale, for instance, have a larger brain than humans, so, logically, they should have at least an equal degree of consciousness. And even if it becomes possible to define where consciousness begins and ends, many creatures with a relatively 'simple' brain may still possess it.

Emerging Consciousness

The second theory suggests that awareness is something that 'just happens' in a complex computing system: it is an 'emergent property'. It is best understood by visualizing the brain as a phenomenally complex system of tiny interlinked computers, which shuffle huge amounts of information between themselves, each one modifying it slightly, so that the by-product of trying to make sense of the world is awareness. So consciousness emerges from processing vast amounts of information. Clearly, once again this 'emergent property' is unlikely to have arisen solely in man.

The Universal Mind

The third theory suggests that consciousness is a fundamental property of the universe in which we live. That consciousness arises as soon as the conditions are ripe. It is an inherent part of the underlying forces that govern the universe. All that we observe in the universe is a product of the interactions between these fundamental forces that mould space, time and matter. Like these underlying physical forces, consciousness is simply part of the way the universe functions. Consciousness, like gravity, manifests itself under the appropriate conditions. The ramifications of this theory can be quite enormous. If consciousness is a fundamental part of the way the universe functions, even quite simple brains could experience it. Even insects would have a faint stirring of awareness. The more complex the brain, though, the presumed greater intensity of consciousness. Once again, this theory furnishes no clues as to where awareness begins and ends but instead suggests that it may be vastly more common than we think.

Professor Stephen Clark says, 'Consciousness seems to be pervasive. Creatures are responsive. What they're responsive to, how good their memories are, and what exactly their quasi-conceptual network is, seems to be just grubbing at the problem. We may be missing the point entirely. We have to ask: What sort of universe is this? Is it made solely from matter and then this very odd thing 'consciousness' somehow magically turns up? I don't think that is true. It must be all pervasive.'

In a universe where consciousness is common the question, according to Stephen Clark, is not, Do animals possess it? but How do we live with it? 'Assuming we're going to go on living and we're going to go on making use of each other – imposing costs on each other – then the best we can manage, and still feel reasonably good about it, is if we try and impose costs that are not too extreme and the ones that we accept are the price we pay for living. Minimizing those costs and living according to the rules that, as it were, can be agreed by everybody participating, then becomes paramount.'

Rational Animals

There is a strong basis for believing that many animals are conscious, that they are more than automatons driven by complex reflexes. But many assume that animals have little or no capacity for rational thought. Because the power to reason is one of humanity's most powerful traits, it is convenient to separate man from the rest of creation on this basis. The separation of man from beast is the key to denying rights to animals and allowing them to be used for humankind's purposes. But there is little evidence to suggest that many animals are not rational – just the belief that humans are different and, therefore, the only creatures capable of reasoning. Animals are presumed to be guided by conditioning and instinct, as, of course, until recently were women and non-whites. Many psychologists reject the notion that animals are capable of rational thought but instead assert that they learn to react in a certain way because a reward is produced. In short, animals become 'trained' to react, whether by man or nature.[38] Yet this idea could also be applied to humans: perhaps our complex brains allow us to be trained better, by each other and society, so that we give only the appearance of rational behaviour. But would we know? Surely our fellow humans would lack the rationality to unmask the deception and reveal the truth.

Other psychologists object to animal rationality on the grounds that most behaviour is the result of an interplay between basic urges and instincts. Examples amongst 'lower' creatures are easy to come by: bees, for instance, often show complex behaviour when they 'dance' to tell their sisters where a good food source is to be found. The dance conveys vital information about the location of the food source; this language appears complex and conveys information efficiently. But this apparently rational behaviour is easily unmasked: if a bee's antennae are stimulated in the right way, it will begin to dance even if no other bees are present. It is simply a 'tropism', a type of reflex action. Many psychologists believe that even quite complex behaviour in 'higher' animals is the result of such a reflex, provided by their bigger brains. The theory suggests that a brain stores reflexes akin to small computer programmes (or sub-routines), which when activated by certain stimuli perform specific tasks: insects with small brains have comparatively few sub-routines, which are easily exposed. Perhaps, therefore, bigger brains of higher animals have a wider range of sub-routines that produces the appearance of rational behaviour. According to Professor Daniel Dennett, of Tufts University, however, it is impossible to add enough sub-routines to cope with every conceivable situation. He says: 'There will always be room for yet one more set of conditions in which the rigidly working out of response will be unmasked, however long we spend improving the system. Long after the . . . behaviour has become so perspicacious that we would not think of calling it tropistic, the fundamental nature of the systems controlling it will not have changed; it will just be more complex. In this sense any behaviour controlled by a finite system must be tropistic.'[39] If the traditional animal-behaviour experts are correct, we would be able easily to spot the loopholes in even the most complex of animal-behaviour programmes. We have not looked in farm animals, of course: we have made the assumption that they lack rationality and consciousness because it suits us to do so.

Life on earth has been evolving for hundreds of millions of years and it is possible that rationality and consciousness emerged in animals out of the ever-increasing complexity and variety of programming in their brains. If Professor Clark is correct, they arose because the universe functions that way. Whatever the basis for it, Darwin readily accepted that animals are capable of rational thought: for him the question was not whether they could reason but the degree to which they could do so. For him it was so obvious that they are capable of rational thought that he was often dismissive of those who ridiculed the concept. In *Created From Animals*, James Rachels quotes the writings of Darwin:

> So many facts have been recorded in various works shewing that animals possess some degree of reason, that I will here give only two or three instances, authenticated by Rengger, and relating to American monkeys, which stand low in their order. He states that when he first gave eggs to his monkeys, they smashed them and thus lost much of their contents; afterwards they gently hit one end against some hard body, and picked off the bits of shell with their fingers. After cutting themselves only once with any sharp tool, they would not touch it again, or would handle it with the greatest care. Lumps of sugar were often given to them wrapped up in paper; and Rengger sometimes put a live wasp in the paper, so that in hastily unfolding it they got stung; after this had once happened, they always first held the packet to their ears to detect any movement within. Anyone who is not convinced by such facts as these, and by what he may observe with his own dogs, that animals can reason, would not be convinced by anything I could add.

Research at Harvard University and Radcliffe College in Cambridge, Massachusetts, reported in 1996 goes even further and demonstrates that young rhesus monkeys have greater mathematical abilities than human children of the same age: they performed tests on the monkeys similar to those used to measure mathematical ability in human infants. The results were surprising to say the least. Professor Marc Hauser tested the young monkeys by showing them one or two aubergines at a time and then hiding them behind a screen. When the scientists tried to fool them by changing the number of vegetables, the monkeys were aware of the differences. Professor Hauser said the animals 'pass the tests that human infants don't seem to pass until they have the linguistic labels for the objects. Although language facilitates mathematics, it is not critical.' The work has also been repeated with cotton-top tamarin monkeys with the same results and indicates that mathematical skills exist without the need for training. But, more importantly, according to Professor Hauser: 'For the first time we have techniques that allow us to compare cognitive abilities across species.'[40]

But what of those species most commonly exploited by man? Little research has been performed to try to discover the degree of rationality in farm animals. The reason is straightforward: most research, especially agricultural research, has specific objectives, which are generally focused on making plants and animals more useful to humanity. 'Pure' research, with its only aim the pursuit of knowledge for its own sake, is rarely carried out. Virtually all research on animal rationality and behaviour is conducted with such 'tied money', which severely constrains the work of experimenters. In addition, according to Dr Mike Mendl, a farm-animal behaviour expert at the Scottish Agriculture College, 'Many researchers have not thought about doing such research. Many believe it's not possible to see rationality in farm animals.' It is not a conspiracy, neither are many researchers aware of how their work is focused away from pure to applied research. The system just works like that and acts against the interests of both science and animals.

There is also the problem of defining the boundaries of rationality, which are unique to each species. Animals and humans have evolved to solve the problems most likely to confront them in their natural environment. But some general principles can be established and rationality can be divided broadly into two levels: high and low.

Low-level rationality is the ability to link events with, say, a reward – for example, pressing a button to release a favoured food from a dispenser. A good memory is considered essential to low-level rationality as is the ability to manipulate objects in the brain to solve problems, such as 'maps' of the immediate environment, and to recognize the flow of time.

High-level rationality encompasses the features of low-level, but also includes such features as the ability to make intuitive leaps, to empathize with other animals and identify with them and their surroundings, complex communication – not necessarily by human-type language – and flexible behaviour. There is no sharp dividing line between high- and low-level rationality. The divisions are entirely artificial to allow experimenters to understand complex animal behaviour.

Low-level problem solving has been studied in farm animals. Pigs learn quickly to control the temperature of their environment by poking their snouts through a light beam linked to a thermostat; this experiment revealed that they prefer their surroundings to be cooler than had been previously suspected. Pigs and chickens are good at identifying the behaviour of their fellow animals and notice quickly if they find food. Sheep can pick out shapes, if they receive a reward, while pigs are acutely sensitive to smells. Both pigs and sheep have good memories for locations of food sources. Pigs are also very good at judging time: if they are used to receiving a stimulus at regular intervals they become agitated if it stops suddenly. Memory, awareness of time and events are low-level abilities, but they are all essential cornerstones of rationality and consciousness.

High-level abilities have rarely been sought in farm animals but Dr Mike Mendl of the Scottish Agriculture College, is currently seeking funds to investigate high-level rationality in pigs. Other researchers, working on Vietnamese pot-bellied pigs, have discovered that they can communicate using symbols and shapes. They do not have the ability to manipulate language like humans – that requires a syntactical structure – but for the first time scientists have studied farm animals to determine whether they can convey information between themselves: previous work has been largely confined to primates, dolphins and whales. Rats and primates are very good at piecing together scraps of information and making intuitive leaps: if rats in a maze normally travel from position A to C via B and B is blocked, they will move directly to C. Experiments of this type show that they have a good memory, a mental map, probably an awareness of self, and also the ability to manipulate that information intelligently to arrive at a rapid conclusion. Once again, such experiments have not been carried out with farm creatures.

One interesting area of research is the study of empathy in the chicken – perhaps the least intelligent of farm animals. If a hen is taught that red seeds taste good and blue ones bad and her chicks are taught the opposite, the hen becomes agitated when she sees her chicks eating the 'bad' seeds. She can transpose her own thoughts onto her chicks and understand their predicament: in humans this is called empathy, and is a relatively high-level ability.

Animal Communication

It is often claimed that humans are the only species to possess language but, as Stephen Pinker, from the Massachusetts Institute of Technology points out, many animals communicate perfectly satisfactorily – spoken language just happens to be our way. Darwin believed that complex communication was common throughout the animal kingdom and postulated how spoken language could have evolved in humans. He wrote:

> I cannot doubt that language owes its origins to the imitation and modification of various natural sounds, the voices of other animals, and man's own instinctive cries, aided by signs and gestures . . . we may conclude from a widely-spread analogy that this power would have been especially exerted during the courtship of the sexes, – would have expressed various emotions, such as love, jealousy, triumph, – and would have served as a challenge to rivals. It is, therefore, probable that the imitation of musical cries by articulate sounds may have given rise to words expressive of various complex emotions . . . [m]ay not some unusually wise ape-like animal have imitated the growl of a beast of prey, and thus told his fellow-monkeys the nature of the expected danger? This would have been the first step in the formation of language.

One useful feature of our complex spoken language is that it allows us to formulate a complex series of rational thoughts. It also allows the transmission of information from one generation to the next. But, on closer inspection, many species pass down information from one generation to the next, if only by mothers demonstrating to their offspring how a problem may be solved. Once again, at this level, the difference between the communication of beasts and men is of degree not of kind. But what about complex abstract thought? This appears to be the sole preserve of humans. It

177

is impossible to determine if language guides thought but it follows that as animals lack the ability to communicate abstract thoughts they simply cannot think them in the first place. Either language is, in essence, thought, or thought is expressed through language. Might it not be that thought does not occur in one's native language but in a different type of communication? If this is so, language would not be required to rationalize and solve complex problems. However it would take a complex means of communication to transfer those thoughts meaningfully to another. Even without a complex spoken language, many animals appear perfectly capable of solving difficult problems, even those involving some abstract thought. Jane Goodall has observed wild chimpanzees displaying the ability to plan for the future, visualize a problem and solve it: they carefully selected tools and set off to visit a favourite termite mound. Not very impressive, perhaps, but it takes abstract thought to select an appropriate tool, to travel to the termite mound and to use the tool effectively.

Experiments carried out in the 1960s and 1970s appeared to show that chimpanzees could use the American sign language used by the deaf. It was claimed that Washoe, a chimpanzee trained by Roger Fouts at the University of Nevada, could ask and answer questions as well as improvise phrases he had not been taught. Following this success, others rushed to duplicate the work but no animal, it appears, has so far been trained to communicate meaningfully with a human. There is also a gathering body of evidence that appears to show that the early successes were the result of feedback between the monkeys and the experimenters. The animals may simply have been responding to the body language of their human trainers, which, of course, is a form of communication. Or perhaps they were merely giving out stock answers in response to a reward – that they were not using real language but mimicking the trainers' behaviour. However, more recent work carried out by Professor Sue Savage-Rumbaugh, from the Yerkes Primate Centre at Emory University in Atlanta, Georgia, does seem to indicate that pygmy chimpanzees may be capable of learning and using language meaningfully. What's more, she claims that wild chimps may also have their own language.

Professor Savage-Rumbaugh's work centred on teaching chimpanzees to communicate via symbols on a board. As each symbol was touched, it lit up and could therefore be used as a primitive form of language. One pygmy chimp, called Kanzy, learned the symbols almost by accident: Professor Savage-Rumbaugh was trying to teach his mother to communicate, virtually without success, but when Kanzy was separated from her he began to use the symbols that she had been taught. He had learned them entirely by himself. Professor Savage-Rumbaugh says that because Kanzy learned language unexpectedly and because she had not looked for such a result, anthropomorphism cannot be attributed to her findings, which suggested to her that 'They are probably doing it in the wild.' She goes on: 'The leap is very small. The problem is that we've been so anthropocentric that we've gone out into the wild and we've said, "Where is human language? What's your name for this and your name for that?" If an ape doesn't point at something and tell you the name for it you conclude automatically that it has no language. What we don't do is look at how language really functions in human beings. Its a social, co-ordinating and organizing vector. Everybody who's watched apes in the wild says there's a tremendous amount of social co-ordination. We've not looked in that arena. We've not dared to look for language. We want not to find it there. That's the problem.'[41]

Moral Animals

The one convincing argument to set humanity apart from the rest of creation is the claim that humans are the only moral animals. Humans show compassion for the weak, the young, the elderly, and, occasionally, for members of other species. In theory humans have complex codes of ethics that distinguish between 'right and wrong'. Humans also have a conscience. Morality is, in essence, an understanding that allows one animal to appreciate and respect the interests of another.

In fact, many humans are far from moral agents. Humans routinely slaughter their own kind for pleasure and profit. They oppress other humans of different cultures and races, males oppress females, and compassion to many is just an empty word. Even conscience has its price. If an objective view is taken, human morality is a fluid concept with little substance. But if animals could be legitimately denied rights because they lack the concept of morality, a truly moral human would not house them poorly, cruelly mistreat them, hunt them for fun, inject them with poisons for profit or eat them for pleasure. In this sense, most humans are not moral animals and therefore should be denied rights on the same basis.

But animal-rights philosophy does not depend on animals being moral agents, but on their being sufficiently like us to suffer pain. We do not hold children or the mentally handicapped responsible for their own actions, neither do we mistreat them because they do not have a well-developed sense of morality: they are not mistreated because they are capable of suffering. The same should be true for animals. Non-human animals are capable of suffering and our impact on them, therefore, should be minimized. Some philosophers, notably Professor Andrew Linzey, argue that we should go further: 'I suggest that the weak and defenceless should be given not equal, but greater consideration. The weak should have moral priority.'

Nevertheless, despite our long history of man's inhumanity to man, we do at least aspire to morality. But is this true for non-human animals? Once again there has been little research into morality in animals. This is hardly surprising. The last thing a scientist wants to discover is the animal on which he has been experimenting is a rational, moral creature. For many, though, the concept is laughable. But there have been a few revealing experiments. The work has been confined, again, to primates, our closest relatives.

The pinnacle of human morality is altruism: the willingness to sacrifice one's own interests for another's. Research performed at the Northwestern Medical School in the mid-1960s indicates that rhesus monkeys are altruistic.[42] The experiments, reported in psychological journals in 1964, were grim for the animals involved. They were placed in boxes with steel floors designed to give them a strong electric shock. Whether or not they received a shock depended on another monkey. When the second monkey pulled a chain to deliver food, the first received a shock: thus the second monkey obtained food at the expense of the first, who received a shock in full view of the second. After numerous painful trails, the experimenters concluded that the monkeys would consistently suffer hunger rather than cause pain to another. In the name of scientific rigour, numerous variations on the experiments were performed, and the researchers found that the animals' reluctance to injure another did not depend on the sufferer's position in a hierarchy, nor on its sex. They also ruled out the effect of an increased noise level from the screams of the monkeys. Screams were referred to as 'vocalization' – they needed to fend off allegations of anthropomorphism. The end result of the painful exercise was that it demonstrated that rhesus monkeys appeared to show altruism. According to Professor Steven Clark, one revealing feature of the experiment is that 'The one thing the psychologists in question didn't mention is that they themselves went right on doing the experiments, which is rather suggestive.'

Another series of experiments performed around the same time on humans revealed quite the opposite. One man was asked to deliver an electric shock each time another person answered a question incorrectly. The second did not actually receive a shock: he was an actor with a very loud scream. The rather depressing result was that as long as the person delivering the shock was assured that there would be no legal consequences for himself, he continued to deliver shocks of escalating intensity. Although the findings of the experiment were by no means conclusive, it seems that for many humans altruism is as elusive as it is presumed to be in animals.

More recent work carried out at the Yerkes Primate Centre indicates that chimpanzees also possess the emotional framework necessary for morality.[43] Frans de Waal has spent many years studying chimp behaviour and reported in 1996 that they share food with their companions and care for others around them. They do this, he says, with the implicit understanding that others will return the favours. 'With reciprocity and obligation we are getting very close to rights, and the concept of fairness is not far behind,' he says. His painstaking work reveals that the most generous chimps were the most likely to be invited to share the food of others while the stingy ones were often rebuffed aggressively. This pattern of generosity and reward did not reflect the individuals' social status in the group. The 'rules' were also enforced by most individuals in the group, rather than by the few dominant males. The chimp behaviour is a form of justice enforced by the whole group. This capacity for systematic revenge, de Waal says, is one of the cornerstones of morality: 'Justice can be construed as a form of controlled revenge.' In the chimps, it extended further than sharing food: a chimp beaten in a fight by another was actively sought out and consoled with a hug by other members of the group. Recognizing and empathizing with another's distress requires a well-developed sense of self – another central feature of morality and the cornerstone of sentience.

The work with chimps also has happy ramifications for human nature: it suggests that morality may not only be an integral part of chimp nature but also of human nature. The conventional view is that morality is the result of religion and social pressures, with raw human nature being nasty and brutish: 'Natural selection is harsh. Natural selection is selfish but its products don't have to be that way,' says de Waal.

Rights and Duties

Some philosophers claim that animals cannot have rights because they are incapable of consenting to a contract that confers duties upon them. Rights and duties are equivalent and cannot be separated. This argument is akin to that used to separate humans from animals on the basis of morality. The core of the philosophy is the reciprocal arrangement originally formulated by the Stoics more than two millennia ago. When philosophers talk of contracts they are referring to a series of unwritten rules on which 'reasonable' people can agree: As an example, an individual is duty-bound not to torture another because that person has agreed, unwittingly or not, not to torture others. Contract theory is based upon brutal self-interest between consenting individuals. In a cynical era this approach appears logical and clear-cut but on closer examination it is far from being so. Rights are also afforded to people incapable of consenting to a contract: we do not torture infant humans or the mentally handicapped even though they have not consented to a contract. Neither do we hold them responsible for their own actions. Animal rights are an extension of these basic human rights because it is logical for them to be so. Animal-rights philosophy is based primarily on a creature's capacity to feel pain because it is sentient.

Philosophers have employed various means to clear these logical hurdles in contract theories of ethics and deny rights to animals. They claim that the handicapped, for instance, can be afforded rights because they belong to a species that would normally consent to a contract and therefore possess rights. A child would ordinarily grow, become an adult and in time consent to the contract conferring both rights and duties. These are morally justifiable positions from an animal-rights perspective, but are illogical and inconsistent from the viewpoint of contract theory. Contract theorists can only assert such rights on the basis that they belong to a species that would normally possess the ability to consent to a social contract.

The provisos that are required by contract theory to encompass the young, old and the handicapped means there is a fundamental inconsistency with the theory. The ethics are simply another way that humans use to exclude a group from the circle of compassion. Humankind has selected a feature that it feels it alone possesses and which allows the exclusion of animals. It's convenient. It means that animals can be tortured, eaten, hunted for fun and experimented upon because they do not have a feature that mankind has deemed necessary to join the rights bearing club. Before animal-rights philosophy was formulated there were few serious challenges except from theologians who claimed that mankind was special because God had deemed it to be so. Now, the evolving animal-rights philosophy exposes it for what it is – a cosy ethical system designed for the needs of humanity.

13

The Future

There is a clear, logical case for animals to be accorded basic rights, strengthened by an awareness of the abuses perpetrated on them. And on the grounds of common decency, a system that inflicts appalling suffering on around 720 million creatures per year, as the meat industry does, should be opposed on principle. As a comparison, 'only' about 2 million experimental animals are killed annually.

Professor Peter Singer, in *Animal Liberation*, and James Rachels, in *Created from Animals*, have popularized the most realistic view of animal liberation: instead of formulating a rigid set of codes, like a constitution, with a list of rights that must not be violated, their starting principles are based on the equal consideration of interests, which grew from the work of Dr Richard Ryder, Brigid Brophy and other members of the Oxford Group of philosophers. They say that where animal and human interests are in conflict, due weight must be given to the interests of the non-human animal.

This idea fits in with one of the most pervasive influences on modern society, Utilitarianism: the philosophy of trying to achieve the greatest good for the greatest number of people, which is reflected throughout society, from the idea of the 'public interest' through to maximizing economic growth to boost individual wealth. It sounds a worthy philosophy. But it has another, darker side: because animals are considered to have no interests, they cannot be taken into consideration and, therefore, the animal can be used and abused at will. Yet if Darwin's work is accepted Utilitarianism can be extended to include the interests of animals: if animals are not fundamentally different for humans and can suffer, their interests can be legitimately taken into account and factored into the equation to try to achieve the greatest degree of happiness to the greatest number. But Utilitarianism is not entirely satisfactory even when applied strictly to humans: the suffering of a gang-rape victim could theoretically be justified on the grounds that the pleasure gained by several perpetrators outweighs the suffering of one victim. Dr Richard Ryder has modified this philosophy by concentrating on the individual because it is the *individual* who suffers not the tribe, sex or species. For this reason, he says, pains and pleasures cannot be aggregated and traded off against each other between individuals, as occurs in Utilitarianism: 'My pain and the pain of others are in different categories; you cannot add or subtract them from each other. They are worlds apart. For example, inflicting 100 units of pain on one individual is, in my opinion, far worse than inflicting a single unit of pain on a thousand or a million individuals, even though the total of pain in the latter case is far greater. In any situation we should thus concern ourselves primarily with the pain of the individual who is the maximum sufferer. It does not matter, morally speaking, who or what the maximum sufferer is – whether human, non-human or machine. Pain is pain regardless of its host.'

So where does this leave the rights of animals?

The only way forward is to formulate a code of ethics that guarantees the rights of both human and non-human animals, which should not be violated except in the most pressing circumstances. Animals must be seen for what they are: sentient creatures capable of suffering. It follows that rights for animals should not be bestowed on animals by benevolent humans but should simply be recognized as they are in humans. In practice this means that whenever human and animal interests come into conflict due weight must be given to the interests of the animal. Animals must no longer be seen as a utility for human ends, but as an end in themselves with legitimate lives to lead. Basic animal rights – to life, freedom and happiness – must not be violated for human expediency. Where human and non-human animal interests overlap, then equal interests have equal value. It is, of necessity, a fluid philosophy: it is not possible to weigh precisely the interests of individuals of our own species, let alone members of another. But it does provide a strong pointer for minimizing cruelty both to our fellow humans and the rest of creation.

There are many clear examples where animals are abused for no good reason: cosmetic and other product testing, for example, can never be justified because they inflict excruciating pain on large numbers of creatures for a trivial end result. Nor can fox-hunting or hare-coursing ever be considered as anything other than an outrage. Even the vast majority of medical research cannot be justified because animals are generally used for trivial reasons. At first glance, this approach, called 'moral individualism', where each case is judged on its own merits, seems very imprecise, but it is in reality far from being so. The main problems appear in the middle ground, where values and interests have to be weighed carefully: how can the value of, say, an improved treatment for asthmatics be compared to the suffering that other sentient creatures must undergo in a research laboratory to provide it? It cannot. The same problems occur when dealing with human rights. Consider the situation of ten men trapped below the waterline of a sinking ship: does the captain seal them below the waterline, condemning the men to death, and in the process save thirty lives? Or, does he allow the men to escape, the ship to sink and risk even more lives? A wise captain would seal the bulkheads and trap the men. Occasionally stark decisions have to be taken. The same will be true with animal rights. Some theorists claim that life, the most basic right of all, is sacrosanct. On closer inspection this is a great ideal but plainly wrong. The previous example of the sinking ship shows quite clearly that the life of an individual human often has to be weighed against the lives of others. The waiting lists for hospital beds is yet another example. Everywhere we look a value is put on human life. This will clearly be true for animal life too.

But the biggest single animal killer – the meat industry – is not in the middle ground. Suffering is inflicted for the trivial end-product of flesh. Sentient creatures are killed by the hundred million to satisfy human appetites. When the suffering of the animals is compared to the pleasure humans gain from eating their flesh, the meat industry could not stand the weight of Utilitarian philosophy, let alone the stricter values imposed by moral individualism. Once it is realized that animals are sentient creatures with feelings and rights, the sufferings imposed by the meat industry can never be justified.

The first step towards reversing the cruelty is the most personal political statement of all: ceasing to buy the products of the industry. Those involved in it do not need our approval to exploit animals but they certainly need our money. Without a ready market the industry will collapse. According to Professor Andrew Linzey, the key is a policy of progressive disengagement from the industry.

Vegetarianism is the first step and the second is to join the campaign to improve treatment of existing farm animals across

Europe by amending the Treaty of Rome, and the third step must be the adoption of a vegan lifestyle, which makes no use of any animal products, including dairy produce and leather.

A Vegan Utopia?

Animal rights is a classic slippery-slope argument: once one step has been taken the next follows logically. There can be no turning back. For this reason animal-rights philosophy terrifies governments. There can be no appeasement because the end point appears so radical and will fundamentally alter society.

But the first faltering steps were taken centuries ago when the rights of man were first formulated: slaves were freed, women were emancipated and it is time now to release animals from the cruelty and suffering imposed by humanity. Professor Clark says that once the philosophy becomes integrated into mainstream thought, merely altering patterns of behaviour to minimize suffering will be insufficient: 'Instead, there will need to be a radical transformation of thought which has been with us for so long that we've built almost everything around it. Getting away from that is going to be extremely difficult. It's going to call for a lot of imagination, restraint and changing the way we live. In the end there is no middle ground. Once you begin to move in this direction it's very difficult to justify to oneself everything on which our civilization is founded. We will have to start to become imaginative and begin thinking of ways through the complexities. We can't slip back. The idea that we can all go back to an idyllic past, such as an agricultural or pastoral or nomadic society, is not possible because it was not in the least idyllic and it was also very nasty for the associated animals. We have to do better than that.'

Mark Glover, of Respect for Animals, says that 'in the long run it means a vegan society. You can already see the moves in that direction. You only need to walk into a supermarket to see the massive cultural shift that's taking place. Everywhere you look there are vegetarian and vegan products. They are not doing it out of idealism – they are simply responding to the cultural shift.' To Glover, the rights of animals means 'minimizing our impact on the environment, each other and on non-human animals'. But in the shorter term, even if we just have to muddle through the complexities and make the odd compromise, it's better to be part of the solution than part of the problem.

14

Progressive Disengagement

The most basic right of all is to not end up on someone's fork. Clearly this will not happen for most animals in the foreseeable future, so, instead, those people who wish to make a meaningful contribution to animal welfare must cut the ground from beneath the meat industry. One way is to take action on an individual level and stop buying meat products; another is to take more direct action against the trade; the third is to amend the Treaty of Rome, the cornerstone of the European Union, so that animals are recognized as sentient creatures. At present they are regarded as agricultural products, alongside vegetables, cereals, meat and the 'guts, bladders and stomachs of animals'.[44]

Amending the Treaty is vital: at present community legislation is assessed for its impact on trade, capital, the environment and the people of Europe, but not on animals. This will change only when the Treaty stipulates that the welfare of animals must be considered in all aspects of community legislation. Pressure is growing to make this change. In 1991 a one-million-signature petition calling for just this was presented to the European Parliament. In the same year at the end of the last Intergovernmental Conference, which decides on Treaty amendments, the Declaration on the Protection of Animals was added to the Maastricht Treaty.[45] This stated that:

'The conference calls upon the European Parliament, the Council and the Commission, as well as the Member States, when drafting and implementing Community legislation on the common agricultural policy, transport, the internal market and research, to pay full regard to the welfare requirements of animals.' This declaration was one of intent only, and has been roundly ignored, but it was a vital step along the road to amending the full treaty.

Since then pressure has been building. MEPs now receive more letters on animal welfare issues than on any other subject. In response, since 1993 the European Parliament has said three times that animals should be re-classified as sentient beings and that their welfare should be a fundamental component of community legislation.

Amending the treaty will not be a panacea; it will not destroy the meat trade but will instead steadily erode the worst excesses of the industry. It will become encumbent on policy makers to consider the welfare of animals in all community legislation, just as they presently assess it for its impact on trade, the environment and on the citizens of the Union. If they fail to do so, the welfare groups will be able to overturn their decisions in the European Court of Justice

National laws will also need revision to take account of animal welfare, and, in time, enforcement of rules will have to be tightened up, which will improve the lot of the average animal across Europe and at home.

New Treaty Article on the Status of Animals

The following is the Treaty article demanded by Compassion in World Farming, the Royal Society for the Prevention of Cruelty to Animals, and Eurogroup for Animal Welfare.

(1) In Article 3:
The following point shall be inserted as one of the activities of the Community.

> '(a) ^{bis} measures to ensure respect for the welfare of animals'

(2) In Article 39 (2):
The following point shall be inserted as a factor to be taken into account in working out the common agricultural policy:

> '(a) ^{bis} the need to ensure respect for the welfare of farm animals'

(3) The following Title and Article shall be inserted:

TITLE XVI ^{bis}
ANIMAL WELFARE
Article 130t ^{bis}

(1) Community policy on agriculture, transport, the internal market and research shall pay full regard to the welfare requirements of the animals used or produced in these sectors.

(2) Live animals, although included in the terms 'goods' or 'products' in the treaty, shall be considered as sentient beings and be treated accordingly in Community legislation.

(3) The Council, acting in accordance with the procedure referred to in Article 189c, shall take decisions in order to achieve the objectives referred to in paragraph 2 of this Article.

(4) The measures adopted pursuant to this Article shall not prevent any Member State from maintaining or introducing more stringent measures to protect the welfare of animals. Such measures must be compatible with this

Treaty. They shall be notified to the
Commission.

The 'Five Freedoms' proposed by the British Farm Animal
Welfare Council will serve as a reference point for ensuring a
minimum standard of animal welfare across Europe. They
are:

The Five Freedoms

(1) Freedom from thirst, hunger and malnutrition:
    animals should have easy access to fresh, clean water
    and adequate nutritious food.

(2) Freedom from discomfort: animals should live in an
    environment suitable for its species including
    adequate shelter and a comfortable rest area.

(3) Freedom from pain, injury and disease: by prevention
    and rapid diagnosis and treatment.

(4) Freedom to express normal behaviour: by providing
    sufficient space, proper facilities and the company of
    their own kind.

(5) Freedom from fear and distress: by ensuring that
    living conditions avoid mental suffering.

Appendices

1

Ten Frequently Asked Questions

(1) Why should animals have rights?

Animal-rights philosophy is based on the understanding that animals, like humans, are conscious, capable of suffering, and are aware of their experience of life. There are no fundamental differences in the functioning of the brains and nervous systems of human and non-human animals; the only differences are ones of degree, not of kind. Non-human animals are conscious and, as Charles Darwin argued, they experience a range of emotions including: anxiety, fear, horror, grief, despair, love, devotion, hatred, anger, contempt, disgust, guilt, pride, patience, surprise, shame, shyness and modesty. But, the key similarity between human and non-human animals is their shared capacity for suffering. As Jeremy Bentham succinctly put it: 'The question is not, can they *reason*? nor can they *talk*? but can they *suffer*?'

Despite the lack of fundamental differences between human and non-human animals, our fellow creatures are denied rights because millennia of philosophical thought appears to justify it. Traditional views on animals originated with the Greek Stoic philosophers of about 300 BC. They formulated the idea that animals cannot make contracts that bind them into a system of rights and duties. In essence, animals do not have rights because they do not have duties. This philosophy taught that animals were fundamentally different from humans and eventually this came to mean that they could be exploited because they held little or no value in comparison to humans. This distinction between human and non-human life is the linchpin that appears to permit animal exploitation. These thoughts later became fused with the Christian and Roman traditions, and the value of animal life was reduced even further. In the seventeenth century the value of animal life reached its low point with René Descartes, who taught that animals were so different from humans that they could not even feel pain. Descartes claimed that the mind and body were wholly different entities. The mind was immaterial in nature whilst the body was simply a complex machine. Humans, because they have a mind as well as a body, could think and feel. Animals, however, were devoid of mind and therefore incapable of feeling pain.

Bentham countered these arguments by claiming that animals could clearly feel pain and went further by suggesting that the ability to suffer was *the* fundamental question. Animals could suffer and they had the right not to suffer. Charles Darwin's theory of evolution effectively killed the Cartesian view of animals but it would take more than a century for the full ramifications of his theory, that human and non-human animals are not fundamentally different, to hit home and give birth to the animal rights movement.

There is only one serious challenge to animal-rights philosophy; contract theory. Some contemporary philosophers concur with the Greek Stoic view that animals cannot have rights because they are incapable of consenting to a contract conferring upon them duties. Rights and duties are equivalent and cannot be separated, they argue. When philosophers talk of contracts they are really referring to a series of unwritten rules that 'reasonable' people can agree on. Contract theory is based upon brutal self-interest between consenting individuals. In a cynical era this approach appears logical and clear-cut but on closer examination it is far from being so, because rights are also afforded to people incapable of consenting to a contract. We do not torture infant humans because they have not consented to a contract; neither do we experiment on the mentally handicapped; nor do we hold them responsible for their own actions.

Philosophers have employed various means to clear these logical hurdles in contract theory and in the process to deny animals their rights. They claim that infants and the handicapped, for instance, can be afforded rights because they belong to a species that would normally consent to a contract and therefore possess rights. This approach is a clear attempt to cover a hole in the theory. If exceptions have to be made in a theory in order to justify it then clearly there is a fundamental flaw in the logic. There are no fundamental flaws in the logic underlying animal-rights philosophy, which accords rights on the basis of the capacity to suffer. If a human, young, old or handicapped, can experience life then they have the right to continue living free of torture or brutal death. The same is true for non-human animals. Animal-rights philosophy is simple, straightforward and logically consistent. Contract theory is not.

(2) What's the difference between the animal welfare and animal rights movements?

The animal welfare movement accepts that non-human animals suffer but tries only to reduce it rather than attempt to end the system that causes it in the first place. There is no acceptance that animals have rights, only that humans have a responsibility to respect their welfare before eating or experimenting upon them By contrast, animal rights groups start from the premise that the exploitation of our fellow creatures is intrinsically wrong and so they set about trying to end the system that causes it. A good example is the ferry boycott organized by Respect for Animals, an animal rights group formerly known as Lynx. This campaign forced the cross-Channel ferry companies to stop carrying calves for veal crates and sheep for slaughter on the Continent. Respect started from the premise that the meat and dairy industries were beyond reform and set about destroying them by tackling the weakest link: when the waste calves of the milk industry were shipped to continental veal crates. Within a few months the trade had collapsed and ports and airports across the country were blockaded by demonstrators. BSE finally killed the trade in 1996.

On the other hand, welfare groups such as the RSPCA started from the premise that veal crates cause unnecessary suffering but that eating the flesh of calves was acceptable. They then lobbied for what they considered to be a humane alternative. From the next century modified veal crates, which give calves slightly more room, will replace the traditional and much hated variety. However, long before this ban is due to come into effect, the BSE crisis plus public outrage from animal rights activists has effectively stopped the export of British calves. This has fundamentally altered the economics of the whole European veal industry with, as yet, unforeseeable consequences.

(3) Many animals kill for food, so why shouldn't we?

Predatory animals must kill others for food but humans, who are naturally either vegetarian or omnivorous, have a choice. We do not need to kill so why should we? We are capable of deducing that killing an intelligent and emotional creature for the pleasure of eating its flesh is wrong. Consider variations of this question to see how groundless it is:

'Many animals steal so why shouldn't we?' or 'Many animals rape so why shouldn't we?' Organizing human society based on certain aspects of animal behaviour wouldn't add greatly to the sum of human happiness.

(4) Surely if animals weren't happy they wouldn't produce meat, milk and eggs?

Unfortunately, this isn't true. Producing eggs, milk and offspring is a purely physiological response. The animals have no choice. Hens have been bred for countless generations to produce eggs, regardless of their state of mind. In cows, milk is produced when they give birth: nature has endowed them with this property and humankind has enhanced it. They are artificially inseminated and have no choice but to carry a calf to term and produce milk when it is born. Incidentally, this question also implies that animals are capable of emotion and rational thought, both of which are central to animal-rights philosophy.

5) What about plants? Don't they have rights?

Animal rights are acknowledged on the basis of animals being able to suffer pain and distress and also because they are the 'subject of a life'. Plants are incapable of suffering because they lack the sensory apparatus to feel pain and reason. They do not have nerves or a brain; they are incapable of reasoning and therefore cannot suffer. Because they lack the attributes that grant human and non-human animals their rights, they cannot have rights on an individual level. This does not mean that humans have the right to chop down the rainforests or to build roads through treasured landscapes. We have a duty of care to the natural world in its entirety but we do not have the same moral duty to individual plants that we owe to our fellow creatures.

(6) Surely keeping grazing animals as meat sources increases the food supply?

Quite the contrary. It is true that in some upland areas the only viable form of farming is sheep farming but, on a world scale, such lands constitute only a very small part of the total. Even in Britain, where sheep rearing in the uplands is an important part of the meat industry, total food production would increase if the uplands were abandoned and the lowlands were turned over solely to crop production. This scenario would have a highly beneficial impact on Britain's countryside and economy. The uplands could revert to their natural state – dense forest – and the lowlands would have a far higher ecological value because the pressure for food production would be greatly reduced. If the whole country converted to a vegan diet, the entire population could survive using only a quarter of the existing farmland. If chemical inputs were also lessened this land requirement would increase slightly but so would its ecological value. So, far from increasing the food supply, the meat industry reduces it and imposes an unnecessary ecological burden on the country.

Keith Acker sums up the arguments from a world perspective in *A Vegetarian Sourcebook*:

Land, energy, and water resources for livestock agriculture range anywhere from 10 to 1000 times greater than those necessary to produce an equivalent amount of plant foods. And livestock agriculture does not merely use these resources, it depletes them. This is a matter of historical record. Most of the world's soil erosion, groundwater depletion, and deforestation – factors now threatening the very basis of our food system – are the result of this particularly destructive form of food production.

Livestock agriculture is also the single greatest cause of world-wide deforestation both historically and currently (between 1967 and 1975, two-thirds of 70 million acres of lost forest went to grazing). Between 1950 and 1975 the area of human-created pastureland in Central America more than doubled, almost all of it at the expense of rain-forests. Although this trend has slowed down, it still continues at an alarming and inexorable pace. Grazing requires large tracts of land and the consequences of over-grazing and soil erosion are very serious ecological problems. By conservative estimates, 60 per cent of all US grasslands are overgrazed, resulting in billions of tons of soil lost each year. The amount of US topsoil lost to date is about 75 per cent, and 85 per cent of that is directly associated with livestock grazing. Overgrazing has been the single largest cause of human-made deserts

(7) Is organic or free-range meat better?

Organic and free-range products are better in humanitarian terms but both still have major drawbacks. Although the rearing conditions are slightly better the animals still have to be transported to market and on to the slaughterhouse. Once there, they will be dispatched with as little care as factory-farmed creatures. Organic, free-range or intensively reared, they're all just warm meat to the slaughterman.

(8) Vegetarians are always so thin and weedy so meat is good for you, isn't it?

There are thin and weedy vegetarians just as there are many fit, strong and healthy ones. The same charge could be levelled at some meat-eaters. In general vegetarians suffer less from cancer and heart disease and tend to live longer, fitter, and some would say, happier lives.

To date the most comprehensive evidence to prove these

points comes from two huge studies conducted in the USA and China. The American study[46] was conducted on Seventh Day Adventists, who are largely vegetarian, and largely non-smoking. Carried out over a twenty-year period, the study concluded that the male Adventists had only a quarter of the normal risk of dying from heart disease while the women carried about one third of the risk. When these death rates were compared with a similar group that did not smoke, their risks of dying from heart disease were still only about half of the American national average. More interestingly, the chances of dying from heart disease were directly related to the amount of meat in the diet.

The China Study[47] produced even more comprehensive results on the dangers of a meat-based diet. The study revealed that only about seven per cent of protein in the Chinese diet comes from animals, compared with about 70 per cent in the West. The Chinese also consume about a fifth more calories than Westerners. It also revealed that milk does not help prevent osteoporosis: most Chinese people consume no milk, and only about half of the calcium that Westerners do; and yet osteoporosis is uncommon. In fact, osteoporosis occurs most commonly in countries with high calcium intakes and where most of the calcium comes from animal sources. Meat was also shown not to help stave off iron-deficient anaemia. The Chinese consume about twice as much iron as Westerners, mostly from plants, and yet anaemia is uncommon.

(9) You're wearing leather shoes and you drink milk. Aren't you a hypocrite when you talk about animal rights?

No. It's better to be part of the solution than part of the problem. Many people feel unable to give up certain animal products like milk and continue to wear the waste products of the meat industry such as leather. While this may make them inconsistent it does not make them care less for animals. Any reduction in meat consumption is saving lives and this can only be applauded. The fact that they are not wholly pure does not make them lesser human beings and does not mean they should give up trying. This argument is purely a red herring designed to bring all people down to the lowest common denominator.

(10) All these animal-rights nutters are only concerned about animals and not people. Why don't they go off and help people for a change?

Yet another fallacy. A brief glance at the history books shows that animal-rights advocates have been central to the fight for human rights. William Wilberforce and Fowell Buxton, among the founders of the RSPCA, were also the leaders of the fight against slavery in the British Empire. Mary Wollstonecraft, who wrote *The Vindication of the Rights of Women*, also produced a collection of short stories designed to encourage children to be kinder to animals. Some of the early American feminists, including Lucy Stone, Amelia Bloomer, Susan B. Anthony and Elizabeth Cady Stanton, were also connected with the vegetarian movement. And in *Animal Liberation* Peter Singer explains:

> In 1874 Henry Bergh, the pioneer of the American animal-welfare societies, was asked to do something about a little animal who had been cruelly beaten. The little animal turned out to be a human child; nevertheless Bergh successfully prosecuted the child's custodian for cruelty to an animal, under a New York animal protection statute that he had drafted and bullied the legislature into passing. Further cases were then brought, and the New York Soci-

ety for the Prevention of Cruelty to Children was set up.
When the news reached Britain, the RSPCA set up a
British counterpart – the National Society for the Prevention of Cruelty to Children. Lord Shaftesbury was one of
the founders of this group. As a leading social reformer,
author of the Factory Acts that put an end to child labour
and fourteen-hour work days, and a notable campaigner
against uncontrolled experimentation and other forms of
cruelty to animals, Shaftesbury, like many other humani-
tarians, clearly refutes the idea that those who care about
non-humans do not care about humans, or that working
for one cause makes it impossible to work for another.

2

A Cost–Benefit Analysis of the Meat Industry

(1) Presumed Benefit to Humans

Cheap and plentiful milk, beef, and veal.

Actual Cost
- Modern cows are made to produce about eight times the 'natural' level of milk; this siphons nutrients from their bodies, leaving them prey to a host of painful and sometimes lethal production diseases.
- Mastitis, laminitis, a painful inflammation of the foot, grass staggers, a nervous affliction, and mad-cow disease all result from overworking milk cows.
- To reduce the profit-sapping effect of disease, farmers constantly dope their animals with a host of drugs and antibiotics.
- To boost beef production, a quarter of British cattle are believed to be doped with cocktails of illegal and dangerous drugs.
- About three million cattle are slaughtered for meat each year.
- Calves are a waste product of the dairy industry; each year about half a million are exported to Continental veal crates (prior to the BSE crisis).

(2) Presumed Benefit to Humans

Cheap and plentiful pork.

Actual Cost

- Fifteen million pigs are slaughtered in Britain each year; about 20 per cent are at least partly conscious while their throats are slit.
- About two thirds of pregnant sows are kept in close confinement. They are frequently chained in stalls so small they cannot turn around.
- Infectious diseases, inevitable in such cramped conditions, are kept at bay by constant doping of the animals with drugs and antibiotics.
- Most young pigs are reared in battery-style cages.
- Bone and joint diseases are at epidemic proportions because the animals are forced to grow faster than their bodies can cope with.

(3) Supposed Benefit to Humans

Cheap and plentiful lamb.

Actual Cost

- Four million lambs die within hours of birth through exposure, sickness and starvation. Another twenty million are slaughtered for the table; a further two million are exported to the Continent for slaughtering; many travel for days without food, water or rest.
- Millions of lambs are castrated and have their tails docked without an anaesthetic, both extremely painful procedures.
- Sheep are beginning to be factory farmed in close confinement and consequently doped with growth-

enhancing drugs and pharmaceuticals.
- Artificial insemination is becoming increasingly common; semen is extracted when an electric shock is applied to the prostate gland after being inserted through the anus.
- Subsidies are radically lowering welfare standards because farmers are paid for the number of animals on the farm, whether, old, sick or dying, rather than for the number of healthy animals that reach the market.

(4) Supposed Benefit to Humans

Cheap and plentiful chickens and eggs.

Actual Cost
- Seven hundred million chickens are slaughtered every year in Britain; millions have their throats slit whilst still conscious.
- Broilers, used for meat, grow too fast for their hearts, lungs and legs and consequently 200 million suffer chronic leg pain; many cannot walk without using their wings for balancing.
- Battery hens, kept in tiny cages giving them as much space as this book when opened out, suffer on average at least one broken bone when they are 'harvested' from their cages and transported to the slaughterhouse.
- They also have their beaks sliced off with red-hot blades to discourage aggression.
- Millions of male chicks are ground up and fed to their sisters each year.
- The females are fed large quantities of antibiotics to boost egg production.

3

The Views of the Main Animal Welfare Groups

(A) Respect for Animals

Unnecessary suffering is wrong and we should strive to end it. Animals have the capacity to feel pain and to suffer. These are facts that only the foolhardy would dispute and these are the simple premises underpinning the objectives and work of Respect for Animals.

Formed from the ashes of the phenomenally successful anti-fur organization Lynx, Respect for Animals campaigns against the fur trade and live exports. Both are cruel, both are wholly unnecessary and both issues inevitably raise questions about the rights of animals.

Every year, tens of millions of animals are killed for the fur on their backs to satisfy the demands of the international fashion industry. No one needs to wear fur yet these animals are caught in the wild, with barbaric steel traps, or raised in captivity under conditions that lead to stereotyped behaviour, self-mutilation and even cannibalism. Fur traders attempt to defend this cruelty with arguments relating to wildlife management – which is impossible with the indiscriminate use of traps – indigenous peoples, whose cultures the fur trade destroyed and who play no significant part in the international trade, and, most incredibly, because it is 'environmentally friendly' although whole species have been wiped out and others introduced into areas where they do not naturally occur in their quest for more skins. The fur trade is driven by the whims of fashion designers and the price of different pelts at the international auction houses. The amount of cruelty and suffering that underlies its profits are unimaginable and inexcusable.

Yet it can be ended.

In 1985, the UK fur trade was vast. Most high-street department stores had fur sections and fur shops were listed in the *Yellow Pages* throughout the country. In the early 1980s there were more than seventy factory fur farms in the UK, in which some half a million animals were bred each year under highly intensive, barren conditions.

Today the retail fur trade in Britain has been decimated and, although the conditions in which the animals are kept have not changed, there are now only around ten factory fur farms. This massive reduction and the astonishing cultural rejection of fur-wearing is an unprecedented success for animals and points to larger changes that could come about.

In the mid-1980s a concerted campaign was launched, aimed at undermining the demand for fur by attacking it at its most vulnerable point: its image. People buy and wear fur because they want to be seen in it and Lynx was set up to attack this simple relationship. Groundbreaking, innovative advertisements were produced – most notably the famous David Bailey photograph of the woman dragging the blood-soaked fur coat – and displayed throughout the country. The effect was dramatic and almost instantaneous. For the first time those buying and selling fur and, more importantly, those who wore fur were confronted with the harsh reality that lay behind the trade's thin veneer of luxury. The trapping methods and the squalor of the factory fur farms were revealed and the public responded.

Opinion polls revealed that more than 70 per cent of the public were against the wearing of fur, which was, in any case, only practised by a small minority, who were ostracized. It became too embarrassing to wear it and fur sales plummeted.

Lynx fell victim to a libel action brought against it by an element of the fur trade and Respect for Animals was formed to continue the campaign and build upon its successes.

In June 1994, Respect for Animals launched another campaign, this time aimed at ending the export of livestock to Europe, an idea that had found expression as long ago as 1957 when the Balfour Report called for 'Slaughter before export'.

Today, each year some 500,000 calves and 2–3 million sheep are exported from Britain and during the 1990s the numbers have increased. They face slaughter in foreign abattoirs or, in the case of most calves exported, incarceration in veal crates – a contemptible system of rearing animals which has been banned in the UK. Many of the animals don't even make it to their intended destinations. Long-distance transport is highly stressful and deaths are not uncommon. The rules that are supposed to govern the journeys are pitifully inadequate, not policed and as a consequence are, to quote the European Commission 'frequently flouted'.

Overwhelming evidence existed as to the lengths of the journeys these animals had to endure and the cruelties inflicted upon them. Yet nothing was happening to end this misery and the British Government steadfastly refused to act. Respect for Animals launched an initiative aimed at dissuading the main ferry companies from taking lorries full of animals to the continent. To their credit they all responded positively and exporters had to find alternative, independent and more expensive ways of crossing the channel. The large profits to be made drove them on, however, and extra-ordinary lengths were taken to enable them to continue with this morally bankrupt trade.

Respect for Animals is determined to see the abolition of live exports and the fur trade. Both issues call out for respect to be shown for the rights of animals.

The list of crimes that we commit against our fellow creatures is obscenely long, but without doubt the greatest cruelty is to be found in the industrialized institutionalized way that we produce animals for food. Since the Second World War the drive to produce more and more for our dinner plates has led to us turning animals into machines – units of production to which we dare not ascribe feelings. But these animals can and do suffer.

The intensification of battery and broiler chicken units, the selective breeding of turkeys so gross they can no longer reproduce without interference, the routine disposal of male chicks and male calves to foreign veal crates, cows that are nothing more than milk machines to be turned into hamburgers after a few years, exhausted by their short lives are all marks of our 'civilized' society. It was Gandhi who wrote in his *The Moral Basis of Vegetarianism*, 'The greatness of a nation and its moral progress can be judged by the way its animals are treated.'

The eating of meat has a historical and cultural significance. It is associated with power, status – even war – and rituals (carving the Sunday joint, for instance), and myths have grown up around it. The modern meat industry exploits these notions in its propaganda to encourage us to eat more whilst glossing over, even hiding, the basic facts about where meat comes from. Through the ages eating other animals has asserted our dominance over the planet and has mirrored our irresponsible destruction of the world around us. It has had tremendous success in adapting consumer-campaigning techniques to win improvements for animals. Being pledged to alleviate animal suffering whenever it can, it cannot nor will it ignore the cruelty endemic in the meat industry. For further information write to: Respect for Animals, PO Box 500, Nottingham, NG1 3AS. Telephone 0115 952 5440

Compassion in World Farming

The Treaty of Rome, the cornerstone of European Union law, classifies animals as goods or agricultural products alongside cans of beans and sacks of potatoes. The inclusion of animals in the same legal category as inanimate objects has helped sanction the harsh way in which many farm animals are treated as they are worked ever harder in the pursuit of cheap food.

Compassion in World Farming is campaigning for animals to be given a new status in the Treaty of Rome as sentient beings, which would recognize that they are not goods or products but living creatures, capable of feeling pain and suffering. Some suggest that the campaign for improved farm-animal welfare is misguided in that it attributes human needs and feelings to animals – indeed, that it aims to treat animals almost as humans. Thus accusation is nonsense: the campaign is directed against farming methods which often: lead to serious health problems and physical pain for the animals involved; and frustrate their natural behaviour. Systems which make it impossible for hens to nest-build or pigs to root must be condemned as unacceptable.

Much of modern animal farming presents a grim picture of abuse. Millions of animals are forced to spend the whole of their lives indoors, kept in barren, overcrowded sheds or cages or, in the case of sows and calves, exported to veal crates, confined in stalls so narrow that they cannot even turn round. Such animals never experience fresh air or daylight until the day they are carted off to the slaughterhouse.

The practice of selective breeding for faster or larger growth has often had disastrous consequences for the health of the animals involved. Turkeys have been bred to develop huge, meaty breasts. They are so misshapen that they can no longer mate naturally, and their heavy upper bodies place such stress on the hips that many turkeys suffer from painful degenerative hip disorders. Selective breeding together with rich diets has led to dairy cows producing an unnaturally large volume of milk. This and poor housing results in many cows suffering from lameness which often results in long-term pain. But perhaps worst of all is the fate of the modern broiler chicken, which is bred to grow so quickly that their legs cannot properly support their overdeveloped bodies. As a result, each year around 180 million chickens suffer from painful, sometimes crippling leg disorders. The heart and lungs are also unable to keep pace with the rapid body growth with some 7 million broilers dying of heart disease each year before they attain slaughter weight at just 6 weeks old.

One of the least-known aspects of modern farming is its reliance on routine mutilations. Each year millions of lambs are castrated, millions of hens and turkeys are debeaked and an unknown number of piglets are tail docked. These painful operations are performed without any anaesthetic. Debeaking and tail docking are carried out to make animals fit factory farming systems. They could readily be avoided by keeping animals in better conditions. Compassion in World Farming believes that it is wrong to cut bits off healthy animals simply to make them more amenable to our purposes. We fully agree with the Farm Animal Welfare Council that it is difficult to give general approval to any system of husbandry that relies on painful mutilations to sustain the system.

The callousness at the heart of modern animal farming is nowhere more clearly illustrated than in the live export trade. Animals exported from Britain are regularly sent on prolonged journeys in overcrowded trucks, frequently with neither food nor water, all too often to be brutally treated during unloading and at slaughter. Transport problems are not confined to large animals. Each year in the UK around 1.5 million chickens die on the journey from the farm to the slaughterhouse. Another 20 million suffer broken bones.

Clearly radical reforms are needed. Some progress has already been made. Thanks largely to campaigns by Compassion in World Farming, veal crates have been banned in the UK and all sow stalls and tethers must be phased out by 1999.

In 1991 Compassion in World Farming presented a petition with over 1 million signatures to the European Parliament, calling for animals to be given a new status in the Treaty of Rome as sentient beings. In 1994 the Parliament fully endorsed the petition and the next year called for the treaty to be strengthened to make concern for animal welfare one of the fundamental principles of the EU. For further information contact: Compassion in World Farming, Charles House, 5a Charles Street, Petersfield, Hants, GU32 3EH. Telephone 01730 264208

Royal Society for the Prevention of Cruelty to Animals (RSPCA)

The RSPCA is the largest and oldest animal welfare organization in the world. Established in 1824, its founders were responsible for the first animal-welfare laws in the UK and the Society has been either directly responsible for or actively involved in the development and implementation of virtually every subsequent law to protect animals. Furthermore, through its support and links with welfare organizations throughout the world, it has had, arguably, a greater impact on animal welfare than any other organization.

Since its humble beginnings, the Society has become a modern and effective force striving within all lawful means to prevent cruelty. It now has more than 300 uniformed inspectors investigating cruelty and rescuing animals, 200 branches run by dedicated volunteers, 250 staff at its Horsham-based HQ and numerous animal centres, clinics and veterinary hospitals across England and Wales.

Throughout its history, the Society's approach to farm-animal-welfare problems has largely been through the work of its inspectorate in the field, dealing with individual cases of cruelty. Interestingly enough, the first RSPCA inspector to work at Smithfield cattle market in London brought the world's first animal-cruelty prosecution for the mistreatment of farm livestock. Today, attending markets is still an important part of the inspectorate's work.

With the development of intensive farming systems, the RSPCA used new approaches to tackle the problems that emerged as a direct result of demand for more plentiful and cheaper food: for example, the move towards keeping animals in cramped or barren surroundings, or breeding programmes that produced animals that naturally developed painful abnormalities. It aims to influence people, either through education programmes devised to improve the skill and understanding of consumers and those directly involved with animals, or by persuading politicians to improve the laws protecting livestock, or funding research to increase understanding of animals' needs and to develop more humane alternatives to certain farming systems. The RSPCA's recent work to establish proper European safeguards governing the transport of livestock was a media campaign to raise public awareness of the welfare problems and to apply pressure on politicians. Although powerful advertising was at the forefront of the campaign, it was supported by highly trained specialists, which included RSPCA undercover inspectors who trailed consignments of livestock across Europe to provide the evidence that convinced the European Commission that existing transport laws were being routinely flouted. They gained access to continental abattoirs and filmed barbaric methods of slaughter. At the same time, the Society's public-relations departments encouraged politicians to support its proposals; its specialist technical and veterinary departments argued the case against long-distance transportation on scientific grounds; and its legal experts challenged the principles of the Treaty of Rome to have farm animals reclassified as sentient creatures.

On European issues, the RSPCA co-operates with leading welfare organizations in other member states of the Community through the Eurogroup for Animal Welfare. Because of the diversity of farming systems and attitudes to animal welfare throughout Europe, reforms have been slow in coming. However, the signs are encouraging and questions over the future of close-confinement systems have moved from whether or not they should be banned to what the time scale should be for their demise.

In the UK, however, progress in certain areas has been more rapid. For example, keeping non-lactating (dry) sows in stalls and tethers will be illegal after the end of 1998. The key factor that encouraged the UK's Agriculture Minister to make this decision in 1991 was that group housing systems for sows were sufficiently well developed that they could replace sow stalls. To help reach this position, the RSPCA had funded a considerable amount of research in high-welfare alternatives, the results of which were directly responsible for strengthening the argument against sow stalls.

Although legislative reforms provide the best long-term security for animal welfare, legislation in itself is a relatively crude tool: certain husbandry methods may be prohibited, but legislation alone cannot guarantee high standards of animal care. In 1994, therefore, disappointed by greater consumer interest in food and farming methods, the RSPCA launched its Freedom Food initiative, which sought to encourage high welfare standards by linking good farmers directly with the consumer. The concept of Freedom Food was to produce detailed welfare standards for the major farm species, to assess and register farmers, hauliers and abattoirs who wished to work to these standards and to encourage retail and catering outlets to sell the food. The standards cover every aspect of an animal's life from birth to slaughter, and are based on advice from a broad range of independent experts on welfare as well as government codes of practice and recommendations. The scheme now includes high welfare standards for pigs, hens, broiler chickens, sheep, and beef and dairy cattle. The range of products is expanding and the number of producers and retail outlets is increasing rapidly.

Recognizing that animal-welfare concerns are growing in importance in the marketing of food, all major retailers are now working towards either Freedom Food or similar schemes. Because of the volume of their sales, the major retail chains are likely to have a key role in food production methods in the future. The only constraint on the extent to which retailers can raise welfare standards is the cost implication. Since public demand for cheap food was directly responsible for many of the welfare problems that developed, public opinion must change before the RSPCA can achieve its ultimate aims: to prevent cruelty and promote kindness to animals. For further information contact: RSPCA, Causeway, Horsham, West Sussex, RH12 1HG, Telephone 01403 264181

Animal Aid

The BSE crisis, which first gripped Europe in the spring of 1996, is merely the most spectacular symptom of a sickness that goes to the heart of commercial meat production in all industrial nations. There is a simple, irreducible formula that explains it: if you exploit, stress and traumatize animals in order to extract the last penny of profit from them, a large number of them will get sick. If people then eat any parts of their bodies, they too risk getting ill.

We at Animal Aid have repeated this simple truth for as many years as we have been in existence. The link between human health and animal welfare is at the heart of our message and yet, when a BSE-type panic surfaces, animal rights and welfare groups tend to find themselves bypassed by the media, as though they have nothing relevant to say.

The spotlight during 1996 was on beef, but, as Danny Penman's account relates, graphically, we could just as well have been fretting over chicken meat. Broilers are, typically, raised 40,000 to each foul-smelling, windowless shed. Seven per cent of these birds die from disease and starvation before they can be slaughtered. They rot where they fall and their remains and excrement from the shed floors are processed and fed back to the next batches of chicks. The trade journal, *Poultry World*, lists ninety-eight 'common' diseases in its annual Disease Directory. And yet people have been running from beef to chicken as a 'healthy' alternative. The disease rate and early mortality rate of pigs is also high. Discerning animals when given a chance, pigs are confined in tight-fitting metal crates, pumped full of drugs and fed foul, powdered meal and all manner of waste, from stale bakery products to bin waste from hospitals and hotels. Almost a fifth of lambs born every year die in their first days, from disease, exposure and malnutrition. Nearly one million breeding ewes die in the fields or the sheds. Excessive use of drugs, not enough basic care, too much exploitation of the ewe's reproductive capacity – these are at the heart of the crisis with sheep. As this book goes to press, the latest worry is that sheep, as well as cattle, could contact and transmit BSE to people.

And so it goes on. The public wants its cheap meat and the scientists, farmers, druggists and politicians have convinced them they can have it. Animal Aid has no secret agenda, no covert plan of action. Its aim is to persuade people, through dynamic campaigning and factually based educational material, to forgo all animal products. This includes meat, dairy produce, fur, leather and wool. Excellent alternatives exist for them all.

Advocating such a course is neither cranky nor economically destructive. Far from it. The status quo, which calls for the 'production' and slaughter of some 700 million animals every year in the UK alone, is not only inhumane – it is unsustainable. We simply cannot manage the volumes of excreta and chemical pollution that the animal-killing industry engenders. Using land to grow crops to feed farmed animals we then eat is also an absurdly inefficient way of providing ourselves with nutrients. We believe passionately that giving up all animal products is the compassionate and healthy option – and one that also offers society a viable economic future.

Animal Aid was founded by a small-town primary school teacher, Jean Pink. Starting out in her bedroom with a small band of helpers and an old duplicating machine, Jean Pink built a national campaign group that went on to develop a world-wide reputation. She achieved her great success through the force of her personality and through the unanswerable case she made against animal exploitation and slaughter.

In the organization's early days, during the late 1970s, the campaigning centred exclusively on vivisection, and there were as many as ten national Animal Aid demonstrations every week. Nowadays the media expect well-turned data and polished arguments, as well as the street-level drama of demos and protests. Equally, local campaigners require a more sophisticated back-up and strategic lead from the centre. Animal Aid has revised its role accordingly, using, most recently, astute 'packages' on the evils of livestock markets, the sheep and poultry trade, the zoo business, the use of animals in warfare experiments, and the squandering of animal lives in tissue testing for medical research. We also have numerous educational initiatives and teaching resources for schools and colleges.

One of our most impressive developments is Market-Watch, a network of groups across the country who monitor their local livestock markets. Their main aims are to prevent animals being violently handled and to ensure that they have access to water.

Animal Aid also stages exhibitions, and offers leaflets, posters and videos. These are designed not just to expose suffering but to promote our Living Without Cruelty ethos. All in all, it is the most complete campaigning and educational programme offered by any national animal rights group in the UK.

Looking to the future, we must prepare ourselves for the biggest battle of all: that of confronting the 'technodocs' and their wealthy backers who, through the application of genetic engineering, are devising ways of exploiting farmed animals that will make today's regimes look affectionate and generous. They herald their plans as though they had the animals' as well as the human consumers' interests at heart. But such people see animals as soul-less and unfeeling – mere products that they can manipulate and dispose of at will. As to the consumers of these genetically modified travesties, BSE is just a foretaste of what lies ahead if the public dares take at face value the self-serving assurances of the meat industry, and the muddled, equivocal, politically influenced pronouncements of goverment-appointed scientists.

For further information, contact Animal Aid, The Old Chapel, Bradford Street, Tonbridge, Kent TN9 1AW.

Other Animal Welfare Groups

Animal Concern, 62 Old Dumbarton Road, Glasgow G3 8RE. Telephone 0141 334 6014

Beauty Without Cruelty, 57 King Henry's Walk, London N1 4NH. Telephone 0171-254 2929

British Hedgehog Preservation Society, Knowbury House, Knowbury, Ludlow, Shropshire SY8 3LQ. Telephone 01584 890287

British Trust For Ornithology, The Nunnery, Thetford, Norfolk IP24 2PU. Telephone 01842 750050

British Union for the Abolition of Vivisection, 16a Crane Grove, Islington, London N7 8LB. Telephone 0171-700 4888

Care for the Wild, 1 Ashfolds, Horsham Road, Rusper, West Sussex RH12 4QX. Telephone 01293 871596

Environmental Investigation Agency, 15 Bowling Green Lane, London EC1R 0BD. Telephone 0171-490 7040

Eurogroup for Animal Welfare, 17 Square Marie-Louise, Bte, B-1040 Brussels, Belgium

Fight Against Animal Cruelty in Europe, 29 Shakespeare Street, Southport, Merseyside PR8 5AB. Telephone 01704 535922

Humane Slaughter Association, 34 Blanche Lane, Potters Bar, Herts EN6 3PA.

Hunt Saboteurs Association, PO Box 1, Carlton, Nottingham NG4 2JY. Telephone 0115 959 0357

International Fund for Animal Welfare, Warren Court, Park Road, Crowborough, East Sussex TN6 2GA.

League Against Cruel Sports, 83–87 Union Street, London SE1 1SG. Telephone 0171-403 6155

London Greenpeace (not related to Greenpeace International) 5 Caledonian Road, London N1 9DX. Telephone 0171-837 7557

National Anti-Vivisection Society, Ravenside, 261 Goldhawk Road, London W12 9PE. Telephone 0181 846 9777

National Federation of Badger Groups, 15 Cloisters House, 8 Battersea Park Road, London SW8 4BG. Telephone 0171-498 3220

People for the Ethical Treatment of Animals, PO Box 3169, London NW1 2JF. Telephone 0171-388 4922

Political Animal Lobby, Warren Court, Park Road, Crowborough, East Sussex TN6 2GA. Telephone 01892 663374

Royal Society for the Protection of Birds (RSPB), The Lodge, Sandy, Bedfordshire SG19 2DL. Telephone 01767 680551

Soil Association, 86 Colston Street, Bristol BS1 5BB. Telephone 01272 290661

Vegan Society, 7 Battle Road, St Leonard's on Sea, East Sussex TN37 7AA. Telephone 01424 427393

Whale and Dolphin Conservation Society, Alexander House, James Street West, Bath BA1 2BT. Telephone 01225 334511

Please note that the author and publisher neither condemn nor condone the work or campaigning styles of any of the groups listed above.

Notes

1 In Peter Wheale and Ruth McNally (eds.), *The Bio Revolution: Cornucopia Pandora's Box?* (Pluto Press, 1990).
2 G. Cronin, 'The development and significance of abnormal stereotypical behavior in tethered sows', Ph.D. thesis, University of Wageningen, Netherlands, p.25.
3 'Assessment of Pig Production Systems', Farm Animal Welfare Council (MAFF, 1988).
4 Interviewed on BBC2's *Horizon*, 'Fast Life in the Food Chain', (1992).
5 K. Dammrich, 'Organ change and damage during stress-morphological diagnosis', in *Biology of Stress in the Farm Animals: an Integrated Approach*, eds. P. R. Wiedkema and P. W. M. Van Adrichem (Martinus Nijhoff, Dordrecht, 1987).
6 'New Guidance on Stunning and Slaughter in Pig Abattoirs', in *Meat Manufacturing and Marketing* (October, 1993), pp.24–6.
7 In Andrew Tyler, *Silence of the Lambs* (Animal Aid, 1995), p.15.
8 David Henderson, of the Animal Diseases Research Association, Edinburgh, speaking at the launch of his video, *Lamb Survival* (Farming Press, 1990).
9 'Castration', *The Sheep Farmer* (Jan/Feb 1994), p.30.
10 'Watery Mouth in Lambs', Animal Diseases Research Association, News sheet No. 10.
11 A. J. F. Webster, 'The Poultry Industry: Have They a Leg to Stand On?', presented at a symposium on the welfare problems of lameness of food animals and equines: the foot, London April 1995.
12 S. C. Kestin, T. G. Knowles, A. E. Tinch and N. G. Gregory, 'Prevalence of leg weakness in broiler chickens and its relationship with genotype', *Veterinary Record*, 131: 190–4.

13 S. C. Kestin, S. J. M. Adams and N. G. Gregory, 'Leg weakness in broiler chickens: a review of studies using gait scoring, published in the proceedings of the Ninth European Poultry Conference (Glasgow 1994), pp.203–6.

14 In *Caring for Livestock*, report of the NFU animal welfare working group (June 1995).

15 C. J. Savory, K. Maros and S. M. Rutter, 'Assessment of hunger in growing broiler breeders in relation to a commercial restricted feeding programme', *Animal Welfare*, 2: 131–52, 1993.

16 *Farmer and Stockbreeder* (January 1982), quoted by Peter Singer in *Animal Liberation* (Thorsons, 1991).

17 In Peter Singer, *Animal Liberation* (Thorsons, 1991).

18 T. G. Knowles and D. M. Broom, 'Limb bone strength and movement in laying hens from different housing systems', *Veterinary Record*, 126: 354–6, 1990.

19 F. D. Thornberry, W. D. Crawley and W. F. Krueger, 'Debeaking: Laying Stock to Control Cannibalism', *Poultry Digest* (May 1975), p.205.

20 Reported in the Animal Welfare Institute Quarterly, Autumn 1987.

21 M. Gentle, 'Beak Trimming in Poultry', *World's Poultry Science Journal*, 42: 268–75, 1986.

22 In Peter Wheale and Ruth McNally (eds), *Animal Genetic Engineering: of Pigs, Oncomice and Men*, (Pluto Press, 1995), p.56.

23 OECD, 'Biotechnology, Agriculture and Food'.

24 J. Hall et al, 'Manipulation of the repertoire of digestive enzymes secreted into the gastrointestinal tract of transgenic mice', *Bio/technology*, 11: 376–9, 1993.

25 R. D. Parmiter et al, 'Dramatic growth of mice that develop from eggs microinjected with metallothionein-growth hormone fusion genes', *Nature*, 300: 611–15, 1982.

26 V. G. Pursel et al, 'Genetic engineering of livestock', *Science*, 244: 1281–88, 1989.

27 OECD, 'Biotechnology, Agriculture and Food'.

28 Dr Tim O'Brien, 'Gene transfer and the welfare of farm animals' (Compassion in World Farming, 1995).

29 K. Ward, 'Transgenic Farm Animals and Enhanced Productivity' in *Animal Genetic Engineering: of Pigs, Oncomice and Men*, (Pluto Press, 1995), p.66.

30 I. G. Hazelton et al, 'Some effects of epidermal growth factor at

three stages of pregnancy in merino ewes', *Australian Journal of Agricultural Research*, 42: 1301–1310, 1991.

31 Animal to Human Transplants: the Ethics of Xenotransplantation', Nuffield Council on Bioethics report, 1996.

32 'The Ethical Implications of Emerging Technologies in the Breeding of Farm Animals', MAFF report, 1995.

33 OECD, 'Biotechnology, Agriculture and Food'.

34 Ibid.

35 P. Cavalieri and P. Singer, eds., *The Great Ape Project: Equality beyond Humanity* (Fourth Estate, 1993), p.12.

36 'On the side of the animals: some contemporary philosophers' view', RSPCA information booklet.

37 'Mind, brain and self-conscious mind', in *Mindwaves*, C. Blakemore and S. Greenfield (eds.) (Blackwell, 1987).

38 In James Rachels, *Created from Animals: the Moral Implications of Darwinism* (OUP, 1991).

39 Ibid.

40 Roger Highfield, 'Maths is Child's Play for Monkeys', *Daily Telegraph*, 21 February 1996.

41 In *The Great Ape Trial* documentary, Channel Four, 1995.

42 Rachels, *Created from Animals*.

43 Bob Holmes, 'Chimps rise above the law of the jungle', *New Scientist*, 17 February 1996.

44 Annex II of the treaty establishing the European Economic Community, Rome, 1957.

45 Declaration on the Protection of Animals attached to the Maastricht Treaty on European Union in 1991.

46 R. L. Phillips, et al, 'Coronary heart disease mortality among Seventh Day Adventists with differing dietary habits: a preliminary report', *American Journal of Clinical Nutrition*, October 1978.

47 Reported by Peter Cox in *The New Why You Don't Need Meat* (Bloomsbury, 1994). See also *The New York Times*, 8 May, 1990.

Bibliography

The Bible: King James version

Clough, Caroline, and Barry Kew, *Animal Welfare Handbook* (Fourth Estate, 1993)

Cox, Peter, *The New Why You Don't Need Meat* (Bloomsbury, 1994)

Linzey, Andrew, *Animal Rights: A Christian Assessment* (SCM Press, 1976)

– *Christianity and the Rights of Animals* (SPCK, 1987)

– *Animal Theology* (SCM Press, 1994)

Masson, Jeffrey, and Susan McCarthy, *When Elephants Weep: The Emotional Lives of Animals* (Vintage, 1996)

Nunn, Chris, *Awareness: What It Is, What It Does* (Routledge, 1996)

OECD, *Biotechnology, Agriculture and Food* (OECD, 1992)

Rachels, James, *Created from Animals: The Moral Implications of Darwinism* (Oxford University Press, 1991)

Searle, John R., *The Rediscovery of the Mind* (Massachusetts Institute of Technology Press, 1992)

Singer, Peter, *Animal Liberation*, 2nd edn, (Thorsons, 1991)

Webster, John, *Animal Welfare: A Cool Eye towards Eden* (Blackwell Science, 1994)

Wheale, Peter, and McNally, Ruth (eds), *The Bio Revolution: Cornucopia or Pandora's Box?* (Pluto Press, 1990)

– *Animal Genetic Engineering: Of Pigs, Oncomice and Men* (Pluto Press, 1995)

Index

Page numbers in bold denote major section/chapter devoted to subject